Uncaged

Black Hills Wolves 25

By
Katalina Leon

This book is a work of fiction. Names, characters, places, and incidents are the products of the author's imagination or used fictitiously. Any resemblance to actual events, locales or persons, living or dead, is entirely coincidental.

Published by
Decadent Publishing Company, LLC

Look for us online at:
www.decadentpublishing.com

~What Others Are Saying ~

Wolf Shifter and a cage fighter, this is a total page turner! ~ Amazon Reviewer

...this is one HOWLING FANGTABULOUS story that you NEED to read!! With Katalina's exceptional gift for writing such captivating stories, having this very personal layer added even more depth to the character, to the story and to the author. ~ Amazon Reviewer

I was absolutely blown away by this book. It's absolutely amazing. I simply cannot put it down. ~ Amazon Reviewer

I just can't get enough of the Black Hills Wolves! ~ Amazon Reviewer

Wow, great mix of action, drama and hotness that kept me at the edge of my seat. Katalina Leon has lots of great story in her book that kept me wanting to know what will happen next! ~ Amazon Reviewer

A beautiful, heartwarming romance, definitely worth a read. ~ Amazon Reviewer

This author is wonderful. The characters are deep and the feelings are heartfelt. I laughed and cried!! ~ Amazon Reviewer

This book is simply amazing couldn't stop reading it until the end. ~ Amazon Reviewer

Dedication

This story is dedicated to my late sister Christy. I was fortunate enough to have Christy spend her last months in my home. During one of our most poignant conversations, she confessed, "I thought my life would have more romance." She had a few intense relationships and lots of drama, but never a loving romance with someone who really cared.

Within a day of her passing, I started writing *Uncaged*, determined to give Christy the protective, understanding hero she never had in real life. I created Mitchell for Christy, but I hope you'll love him too, because we all deserve a hero who can love us as we are.

Chapter One

L ike a loyal companion, Mitchell's heartache never took a day off. Every hour tested his ability to keep it together. The man in him endured loss in silence, while his inner Wolf threatened to burst to the surface, snapping and howling with rage. The only way to quell the beast was to exhaust it. At his childhood home near the Black Hills, he'd wolf-shift and go for a strenuous mountain run until the pain numbed. In an urban environment like Sioux Falls, the training floor of Hank's Hardware Gym provided the perfect option. With his knuckles pressed to the sweat-soaked wrestling mat, he pumped out a brutal set of straight-arm push-ups.

Counting aloud, he fell into trance. "Eighty-seven. Eighty-eight. Eighty-nine." With his triceps burning and breath heavy, a sheen of sweat built on his skin.

When it came to physical training, he'd become inexhaustible. The harder he worked, the stronger he got. The stronger he got, the harder he needed to work. Among fighters his size, his level of speed and agility remained unmatched. Natural aggression made him fearless. Under professional guidance, he'd developed into a monster of feral intensity waiting to be unleashed on the mixed-martial arts world.

"One hundred sixteen. One hundred seventeen."

After his arms melted to jelly, he planned to take a night jog to finish himself off before going home to a lonely rented room to gulp down a meal whirred in a blender.

"Hey, Mitch!" Hank lumbered into the room. Except for an Alpine hairline, he still looked like the champion wrestler he'd been thirty years before—a human torpedo of solid muscle.

With his arms straight and body planked, he paused. Only the closest friends called him "Mitch," and their numbers were few. The previous year, a drunken truck driver on an icy road, took his mother, father, and a kid sister out of the picture. Hank, being the solid Lakota patriarch of the gym community, tried to fill the void.

Mitchell collapsed on the black rubber mat and glowered at him. "What?"

"You're the only guy in the gym. I want to close early and go home to the missus."

Standing, he stretched. "I can lock up."

"But you'd have to drive the keys back to my house so I can open at dawn."

The boss lived on the outskirts of Sioux Falls. His hopes of getting a private hour of kick-drills on the punching bag dropped like a rock. "Why don't you make a second set of keys?"

With his bottom lip out-thrust, he frowned. "Third set of keys. Dude, you keep losing them."

Reaching for a towel, he mopped his face. "You're right. I'm going to call it a night."

Hank was the closest thing he had to family in Sioux Falls, but even he didn't suspect there might be something unusual going on right under his nose.

No way could he risk an admission like, *"I forgot the gym keys were in my pocket when I ran into the river basin to shift by the light of the moon and run around on all fours."* Dodgy comments were certain to get him kicked out or drug tested. "I need to switch shoes. I'll let myself out."

"Thanks." He dug a wallet from his back pocket and pulled out a handful of crinkled bills. "You did a good job changing the belts on the weight machines and cleaning the showers. Why don't you buy yourself a steak?"

Mitch pulled a dark hoodie over his head, covering the damp T-shirt. As he reached for the money, he grumbled, "My landlady has other plans for my cash. She's got me on a peanut butter, jelly, and ramen diet."

"That crap will ruin you!" Hank sputtered with disgust. "Come to dinner on Sunday. We'll talk shop. I want to introduce you to someone who could be a real career maker, Tex Wilkins—"

"Tex Wilkins the MMA promoter?" Mitch whistled.

"I sent him some video of your last match. Lately, he's been going around all the best mixed-discipline gyms and competitions, writing contracts and scooping up the cream. You're young, but you've got talent like I've never seen. No one in your age group has your mass and speed on the natch. These days everybody's injecting some sort of witch's brew, but not you. You're a freak of nature! Mitch, with the right kind of help, you could have it all. I'm talking big time. International travel. Exhibitions. Even the ultimate payday—televised pay-per-view events in Vegas and Tokyo. For a good-looking kid like you, endorsements are a sure thing."

"A manager? You think I'm ready to go pro?" A thrill of terror shot through him. Hank had placed his wildest dreams on a platter then set it all within reach. It made sense. The formidable spirit of the wolf in his blood made him bigger, stronger, and a hell of a lot more intimidating than most eighteen-year-olds. "What will you get out of it?"

"Nothing." Hank's face sagged. "Except bragging rights. I'll get to say, 'Before he was famous, I trained Mitch Waya.' We gotta think of a catchy name for you. How about 'Mitch-Hell'?" He paused. "Too obvious? I wish a fairy-fucking-godmother would make me eighteen again and schedule a meeting with Tex Wilkins, but I ain't complaining. I got a good life. So, are coming on Sunday?"

His heart pounded. "Fuck ya!" Broader horizons beckoned, and he needed to get out of Sioux Falls. "Thanks, man. This means a lot. I want it so bad, I can taste it."

"It won't be easy. You're gonna taste blood in your mouth as well as success." Hank gave his arm a slap. "You deserve a break. Now leave, so I can go home." He wandered out of the room turning off lights in the building. "Don't eat ramen." His voice rumbled from the main floor of the gym. "Spend some of that cash on fresh food. Treat yourself decent."

"Yes, Ma!" He laughed and so did Hank. It

comforted him to know somebody gave a damn.

Hank made a racket near the front door restacking iron weights. "I'm setting the alarm. Mitch, get moving! I want to go home and get laid."

He put on his running shoes and laced them. Gathering his towels, socks, and various sweat-soaked items into a duffel bag, he collected at least two loads of laundry. Drawing his hood up, he braced for the shock of a chill October night greeting damp skin. He pushed the rear fire door open, and shouted, "Good night!"

Striding into the dark parking lot, he made a beeline to his car. He opened the trunk and tossed the bag inside. With quick, hopping steps, he forced blood into his legs and jogged away from the downtown business district toward the Big Sioux River. A brisk run along the Yankton Trail would give him a chance to process Hank's good news.

Could he handle life on the pro circuit?

Running faster, he found his rhythm. The lung-hammering rigors of a hard sprint on a cold night brought him peace. Bursts of moist breath crystalized in the dry air. The scent of the season's first snow teased his senses.

The man in him fell into pace and zoned out while the Wolf inside awoke. Distractions came easy. Sights, scents, sensations were amplified by his wolf-enhanced senses demanding undivided attention. Even an insignificant flicker of movement across a busy street caught and held his eye. To his keen ears errant words muttered below the breath, possessed the force of a scream. Something as simple as the scent of an aroused woman in a movie theater made him want to give chase. The musky stench of another man's sweat in a gym provoked territorial instincts. His biggest problem? Isolation. Few outside the shifter community knew the difficulties of straddling two worlds.

Sometimes the longing for one of his own kind grew so strong, he hallucinated the scent of wolf. Even now, in the frigid air, he thought he caught the familiar whiff of a fellow Wolf. Following the ephemeral trail, he veered away from the pavement and took a shortcut along a gravel alleyway bordering on a silent industrial park. All the warehouses were closed. With no moon, only his wolf-enhanced vision made it possible to run safely in the dark. The alternating *crunch* of footfalls on pavement and grit were calming. His thoughts drifted. The Wolf in him enjoyed the freedom of motion, while activity quieted the pain in his heart.

Just as he passed a reeking trash dumpster— *Bam!* The lid flew open. The unexpected movement was so startling he leaped a foot into the air. A grubby-faced boy wearing a knit cap popped his head out.

"Christ!" He swerved away from the dumpster. "You scared the shit out of me!"

The boy appeared to be about twelve, perhaps younger. The downturn of his generous mouth appeared too disdainful to be childlike. Pale and gaunt, the child had large eyes that reflected a haunted quality. Staring in terror, the kid clambered out of the dumpster and dashed into the shadows between two buildings.

"Wait!" he called after the child. "Are you okay?"

The boy flipped the middle finger then disappeared behind a corner.

"Whatever." Returning to a brisk pace, he continued toward the jogging path ringing the city. On the edge of the riverbank, the water looked inky black. More than a mile passed under his feet when his intuition about the damn boy needled his conscience. The problem needed his attention and could not be ignored.

The boy echoed his situation. If not for the kindness of others, it could have been him climbing out of a dumpster. Last November he'd been at a wrestling match in another county when the news of his family's car accident arrived, along with the warning things looked grim. Barely seventeen at the time, he'd been left with a lot of decisions to make without legal authority or experience to lean on.

Just thinking about it hurt. A sharp but fleeting pain twisted his gut and goaded his conscious to take action. He considered calling Leonora at child services to tell her he'd spotted a boy hiding in the business park. Take-no-nonsense Leonora had been an absolute angel to him. She'd assisted with funeral arrangements, housing, scheduled grief counseling, and made sure a financial settlement from the accident got set in motion. Without her help, he might have been so overwhelmed he would have returned to the dysfunction of the Black Hills Wolf pack, a fate his parents had been adamant to avoid.

Breathing hard against the cold air, he stopped and stared skyward. "This is fucked up." Muttering, he changed course and returned the way he'd come. No way he could continue jogging, knowing a frightened kid roamed an alley on a night sure to drop below freezing.

The dark business park lay straight ahead. High-pitched cries, sounding like a tortured animal, greeted his ears. Muffled groans followed. He sprinted toward the disturbing noises that were definitely human. When he reached the site where he'd last seen the boy, the kid wasn't alone. A large SUV blocked the mouth of the alley. Two men cornered the boy at a dead end. The kid struggled on the ground, moaning as if he'd been punched in the belly.

A dour-faced middle-aged man sat in the driver's side of the vehicle with the window down, observing the scene. Shouting to the two other men, "This isn't the place to deliver sentence. Put Chris in the car. Let's do this somewhere else."

Barely containing his rage at the sight of two burly men bullying a whimpering child, he roared out of the shadows. "Get the fuck away from that kid!"

A balding, heavyset man in his thirties turned to confront him, and shouted, "Who are you? This is a family matter—fuck off!"

His senses tingled. The Wolf within growled, wanting to come on strong. With muscles coiled, he battled the urge to shift and tear their throats out with his fangs. Aiming for the biggest guy, he ran and used his weight like a ramrod. Like a train wreck in slow motion, Baldie went airborne then slammed hard against a cinderblock wall. On impact, he slumped forward, but the punishment continued. Hooking a palm around the man's neck, Mitch drew him downward, using body mass and gravity to advantage. He slammed the guy's face against his raised knee. The crunch of nose cartilage striking bone followed. Taking a final coup, he landed an ax kick on the dude's kidneys and buckled him flat.

"Stop!" A second man, with the same sort of pink jowly face as a pig, pulled a gun and aimed at Mitchell. He hovered near with his arm trembling. Sweat glistened on his brow.

Mitchell froze. The tang of adrenaline rolled off the second assailant's skin. The man reeked of anxiety. The particular scent was familiar. He smelled it often on indecisive opponents who'd lost hope of victory and instead fought desperately for a way out.

"This is none of your business!" Pig-face appeared overwhelmed. With his gaze furtive, he shuffled his feet as if standing on a hot griddle. "Why the fuck did you have to show up?"

Mitchell studied the gunman's chaotic body language, noting hesitation.

"Get back in the car!" a dour-faced man in the SUV bellowed. He revved the engine.

"Don't rush me!" Shaky Gun's attention wandered between the SUV and Mitchell. He looked perplexed. "This dude weighs a ton. Maybe we should kill him somewhere else?"

Baldie's nose bled as he gurgled on the ground. "Jacob, you fucked up. This is way more than I want to be involved in."

Jacob turned on his companion. "So it's my fault? I'm not the jackass who let Chris jump out of a moving car."

Sensing the men were distracted, Mitchell took a subtle step and positioned himself between the SUV and the kid. He shielded the boy who scrambled against the wall. With hands raised in surrender, he summoned his calmest tones. "Don't do this."

"I'm leaving. Now!" the man in the SUV snarled at his companions.

"Wait! I'm coming with you." Baldie tipped his head back and moaned as he struggled to stand. "Goddamnit! Hurts like a son of a bitch! I can't see a fucking thing." Staggering forward, he blindly groped his way toward the SUV and climbed into the backseat.

Jacob tried to grab the boy by the wrist. "Come home, you little shit."

"No!" The kid snatched his hand away then wrapped his arms around his folded knees to sob.

"Cut the crap!" Jacob snatched the child's collar. "We're going home."

Mitchell loomed in Jacob's face. "You better be ready to kill me and commit capital murder because I'm not going to let you take the kid." The Wolf raged to the surface ready to fight. With calculated speed, he knocked the man's arm skyward. The gun discharged into the air with an explosive blast. Pouncing, he knocked Pig-face down and kicked the gun to the end of the alley. With a harsh stomp, he brought his heel down on Jacob's chest, then shoved him away with his foot.

"Goddamn!" Jacob wallowed on his side holding his ribs.

"Jacob," the older man in the SUV screamed. "Get in the car or get left behind."

Rising from the ground wheezing, Jacob limped forward clutching his abdomen. He flopped into the backseat, spewing obscenities. The SUV lurched into gear. With the tires squealing the vehicle rumbled away in a cloud of diesel fumes.

Amped from the intense encounter, Mitchell knelt to check on the boy. The child curled into a ball and hid his face in the crook of his arm. Grubby clothes and the smell of garbage hung heavy, but Mitchell detected something more ominous—the faint scent of blood.

A moment of seething disgust for the men followed. As a child in the Black Hills pack, he'd witnessed violence first hand. A rogue Alpha named Magnum had terrorized the pack with his brutal brand of leadership, sparing no one, not even the women and children. Magnum was the sole reason his parents fled Los Lobos. For their sake, he swore he would never tolerate a bullying Alpha again. He fished his phone out of his pocket, and then hit Leonora's number on the speed dial.

Despite the late hour, she answered immediately. "Mitchell, is everything okay?"

"I'm fine." He sounded shaken. "This call's not for me. During a jog in the business park by the river—"

"By yourself at this time of night? Mitchell that's unwise."

"I found a boy here. Looks like he's about twelve. He's dirty, probably been living on the street for a while. Three men assaulted him. I think he's taken a beating. I left my car in Hank's parking lot. I'm scared to pick him up and move him."

"Stay put. Keep your phone on. My apartment is less than a mile away. I'm going to call an ambulance and meet you there."

Leonora's actions were muffled in the background. All he had to do was wait for the cavalry to arrive. Turning toward the lump of quaking clothes on the ground with a boy inside them, he grazed a hand along the scrawny shoulders, checking for pained reactions or broken bones.

"Help's coming," he muttered in a reassuring voice.

"I don't want help." The child blubbered. "I want a ride home."

"My friend, I'd like a doctor to look at you first. Were those men family?"

The kid blew his nose on his sleeve. "I shouldn't be talking to you."

Feeling alarmed, he made an effort to remain calm. "Why?"

"You're an outsider, one of the riven."

With a featherlight brush of his fingertips, he stroked the side of the child's face. "I'm a what? What am I?"

"Riven. Set apart. One of the hopeless, living outside grace. I mean you live in a city don't you?"

He didn't like the words the child used. Riven, set apart. His secret life as a wolf-shifter left him painfully aware he was different beyond what many could accept. Already lonely, he did not want to be branded hopeless as well. Receiving even incoherent rejection from the child stung.

The kid inched closer and huddled against him. "I'm freezing."

After drawing the hoodie over his head, he wrapped it around the child.

The kid clutched the sweatshirt like a shawl. "They were so scared of you."

The Wolf salivated to sink its teeth into those men. He wiped his mouth on the back of his hand. "They pissed me off. What they were doing is wrong."

"I've never seen them run from anyone. You're like a demon spirit."

He liked that title even less than riven.

"Are you a man or something else?" The child's voice filled with awe. "When you took the gun from Brother Jacob, you didn't look completely human."

"I'm not a demon, if that's what you're thinking." He shook his head. "You have nothing to fear from me. I would never harm an innocent person."

The child's grip on Mitchell's arm tightened. "Then I'll call you my angel."

"My name's Mitchell."

Sirens roared in the distance, drawing closer. Leonora's green sedan rolled into the alleyway first. She jumped out of the car then ran toward them. Looking at the trembling child at his side, she gasped. "You absolutely did the right thing in calling me." A decade of social work etched fanned lines around her compassionate brown eyes. "Mitchell, would you walk to the street and guide the ambulance in? I need to talk to the child in private."

With reluctance, he rose.

The boy reached out with surprising speed and seized onto him. The kid held onto his hand with white knuckles. "Don't go." The words came out a raspy whisper. "Stay close. Protect me."

Leonora observed the gesture in silence.

He patted the delicate hand. "It's okay. I'm coming right back."

Holding tighter, the kid refused to let go. "You're the only one who's ever stood up to him."

Pursing her lips, Leonora leaned over the child. "Who is 'him'?"

With a gentle touch, Mitchell disengaged the child's slender fingers. "Tell Leonora your story. She can help you. She helped me."

"Promise you'll come back." The kid sounded

worried. "I know I'm safe with you."

"I promise I'll come back." He walked to the end of the business park and waited at the curb. The sirens he'd heard earlier were obviously headed somewhere else. It seemed like an eternity before the ambulance appeared with red lights flashing. He directed the driver down the alleyway and followed after they passed.

From a respectful distance, he watched the paramedics raise the child's shirt and palpate the abdomen. With a loud groan, the kid writhed in agony. Everyone looked concerned, which worried him. When Leonora blurted the words "rape kit," Mitchell cringed. Whatever happened to that poor kid was so twisted and wrong.

Medics lifted the child onto a gurney and rolled it toward the ambulance.

"Come here," the kid shouted to Mitchell. "Ride with me!"

Ignoring the demand, the paramedics loaded the child inside, shut the doors, and drove away.

Leonora waved to him. "Mitchell, I'm going to meet them at the hospital. Thank you for doing a kind deed. You can go home now."

Leonora's dismissal felt like a slap in the face.

"I overheard you say that he might be a victim of...." How could he say something so painful? "That he might have been.... Maybe I can be there to support him?" He was already invested in the kid's fate. Walking away now would be heart wrenching.

Leonora's gaze dropped. "Mitchell, he is a she. Christy is a thirteen year-old girl, fourteen in December. From the preliminary examination and from what she told me, she's about six weeks pregnant. They beat her in this alley. Now, it appears she's having a miscarriage. She told me the man driving the SUV claims to be her spiritual 'husband' and goes by the name Reverend Simon. After we stabilize her, I'm going straight to the police to file charges and request a full investigation."

"Holy crap!" The world spun.

"She's running away from some sort of cult. I appreciate your offer of help, but for Christy's comfort, we're going to try to keep men away and win her trust while we help her. There's a lot to sort through. No doubt a high-profile criminal case will follow. Christy is going to need years of therapy and privacy to heal. Do you understand? Don't take it personally."

"Of course I understand." He didn't, but he said it anyway.

"I saw the way she looked at you, clung to your hand. When you walked away, she tried to get up and follow. She kept saying you were the only one who could make her feel safe. Some pretty weird stuff came out of her mouth, too. She said, during the attack, you looked like a fanged beast and that your eyes glowed amber like an 'avenging angel.' Those are her words not mine. What you did for her is wonderful, and I'm not saying anything against it, but we have to practice caution. Christy is very needy, abused, and possibly brainwashed. If she's going to heal and survive, she'll have to learn to trust and rely on a lot of different people, but most of all herself. Another male savior to idolize is the last thing she needs."

His heart sank. "You want me to stay away?"

"For now, yes."

Yet another dark pit opened inside to suck his spirit down. He felt horrible for Christy and worse that he couldn't be there for her. "Will you keep me in the loop? I need to know she's all right."

Leonora searched the pockets of her moss-green quilted coat and pulled out her car keys. "Mitchell, she's a minor. If she's formally assigned to me, I'll have to protect her privacy. Everything beyond this point will be confidential. I'm sorry it has to be that way. You understand."

Once she located the keys, she took a step toward her car. "I have to go. They'll be waiting for me." She loitered for a tense moment. "Even though you turned eighteen in September and you're not technically part of my caseload anymore, I'll always care about you. I'd like to check in now and then. The settlement for your family's accident is pending. It could take months, perhaps another year, but I'll help. Why don't we meet for coffee sometime?"

He paused. The realization hit that someone he leaned on for approval and advice just circled the wagons and left him on the outside. The truth left him feeling like an abandoned child. Caring, stable, and decent Leonora was easily the closest thing to an aunt. He wanted to keep her in his life but sensed she'd already moved on to the next lost soul. "I might not be here much longer."

She tensed with her brows arched. "What are your plans?"

"I'm sure Hank has already mentioned something to you."

"I know my brother dreams big."

Nervous as hell, he shuffled his feet. "Now that I'm eighteen, I can sign my own contracts and travel without a guardian. It totally frees me to take on the mixed-martial arts fight circuit. Hank said I could learn more in one year on the circuit than—"

Leonora threw her hands in the air. "I saw this coming the first day I introduced you to Hank! What about college? Did you ever meet with the tutor I introduced you to? Mitchell you're so smart. If you focused, you could transfer into an engineering program, no problem. There are scholarships available. I'll help you write a grant. Use the money from the settlement to build a future. Please don't mess yourself up in the ring. I've seen that tragedy so many times."

He'd spent every waking hour of the past year training, fighting, and exhausting himself. He would have done anything to dull the emptiness inside except sit still and think. Time spent alone with his thoughts was the enemy. He scheduled each day to the max with endless physical routines to tamp down the suppressed anger continually threatening to erupt. Fighting provided the only safe form of release. He lived for brutal bouts on the sparring mat. The chime of a training bell triggered an inner detonation. He'd become the real Pavlov's dog, trained to rage in a cage. The wounded Wolf in him belonged behind a curtain of steel-mesh, not in a classroom. "I'm meeting with a manger-promoter this Sunday."

Opening the driver's side, she climbed in. "I won't lie. I'm worried for you. Cage fights nearly killed Hank. Promise me you'll think of a fallback plan." Her lips quivered and curled but didn't quite achieve a smile. "And stay in touch." The car window went up, and she was already moving before he could

answer.
    "Good-bye, Leonora."

Chapter Two

Four Years Later

With a sense of purpose, Christy rubbed a glue stick across the back of the last official promotional photo of Mitchell aka "Wail'n Waya." He looked sleek and fierce dressed in black boxing trucks on the steps of a Vegas casino. She pasted the eight-by-ten glossy into her scrapbook chronicling the meteoric rise and fall of Mitchell Waya's MMA career. Flipping the page, she glanced at her favorite picture—Mitchell's smiling face on the label of a sports drink. In this photo, he looked approachable, even kind, an unusual quality in an MMA fighter. The scrapbook had once been a comfort, almost an obsession, but now she needed to move on and put it away.

Turning each page with care, she took a final glance. In the first months of her recovery, she'd hounded Leonora for information about Mitchell so often she'd been banned from asking. Lucky for her, his face started showing up everywhere, even on cable. Without driving Leonora crazy, she could look at him all she liked.

With sweeping dark brows and a dramatic blend of Scottish-Lakota features, Mitchell seemed incapable of taking a bad picture. The media loved him. Young, with the perfect balance of brawn and soft-spoken humility, he drew fans of all ages. Overnight, he became an international hero. His mercurial eyes could convey a sense of playful sweetness one moment and the next a burst of raw ferocity. His unique fighting style was praised as "effortless," "otherworldly," or her favorite quote, "The mixed-martial arts world has never seen a phenomenon like Mitchell Waya. He's a sledgehammer strapped to a fountain pen. The damage is executed with concise elegance."

She gazed at a collectable sport card of a beaming Mitchell holding his championship belt aloft in front of a cheering crowd in Frankfurt, Germany. Or a funny promo shot of Mitchell hamming it up on a train platform in Tokyo. He crouched in the sprinter's position as if preparing to race the train. The caption read: *"Which is faster? The Bullet or Waya?"*

But the good times didn't last. It pained her to look at the next collection of photos. A mega-hyped televised event at the Emperor's Palace, Las Vegas, brought Wail'n Waya's reign to an end. In front of a packed house, Mitchell harmed a man so badly the opponent left the cage a quadriplegic for life. The nerve-severing strike, delivered a split second after a bell, had ruined Mitchell's reputation and caused controversy. With every angle of the tragic incident thoroughly analyzed, an odd feature became apparent. In several frames, Mitchell's face took on a feral animal quality and his eyes glowed amber. Tex Wilkins argued with the press the uncanny effect resulted from multiple flashbulbs and the ambient lights of Vegas, but she knew better.

No longer afraid she'd gone mad—the sad event provided some vindication to the stories she had told to Leonora years ago. There were other witnesses. The world glimpsed the avenging angel doing battle in the cage, too.

The MMA suspended Mitchell from the ring, and an investigation followed. To pass the time, he drank too much and drove too fast—a bad combination that led to wrecking his Lamborghini on a desert highway. With every limb broken, he barely survived.

Worse, sensing his golden goose laid a rotten egg, Tex Wilkins had embezzled Mitchell's earnings and fled. A popular rumor claimed Tex relocated to Argentina.

Her mother, Mara stepped out of the kitchen. "I'm making a BLT for breakfast; would you like one?"

"No thanks, I just finished a bowl of oatmeal."

Mara peered at the photos on the tabletop. "I haven't seen the scrapbook for ages. What made you get it out?" With a gentle touch, she grasped Christy's hand. "We haven't talked about that night in the alleyway for a while, do you need to?"

She closed the scrapbook. "I've got Leonora and two tag-team therapists for that."

A slight smile made Mara's eyes crinkle. "I'm a good listener, too."

"You're a terrific listener and an amazing mom. Sometimes I feel bad that it's always about me and 'the tragedy.' You don't even get to have a private life." She paused. "Do you ever dream sometimes of what it might feel like to not plan your weekdays around seeing a counselor?"

With a soft groan, Mara shook her head. "I'm grateful for the help. I would have been lost."

By bright morning light, she noticed her mother appeared less care-ridden and more beautiful than she'd looked in years. "Me, too, but my God, I want a taste of a normal life. How am I going to get my future moving if all I do is talk about the past? I'd do anything to be free of the boogeyman as a conversation topic. It's all anyone wants to talk about."

"Over time, it will happen. Look at how far we've come. You're already in college, living with a roommate." A nervous laugh spurted past Mara's lips. "I am coping with those changes as best I can. I'm always going to worry, but it's getting easier to let you out of my sight. If I could afford to have a bodyguard follow you on campus, I would."

"I appreciate what everyone has done for me, but sometimes I feel suffocated. I need independence. You know what I would really love?"

"Tell me?"

Capping the glue stick, she tossed it into the plastic craft box. "I want to help someone else."

Mara swept her auburn hair away from her delicate face. "Who? How?"

"Mitchell's been on my mind."

"Poor man. I read he endured months of traction. The media went crazy for his story, but he dropped off the radar. Wherever he is, at least he's alive. With so many people looking for him, you'd think he would have turned up by now."

Chewing her lip. "Leonora knows where he is. I asked her."

"What?"

She steepled her fingers beneath her chin. "Mitchell contacted Leonora when he was released from the hospital."

Leaning across the table, Mara clasped her hands. "Really? He's an adult. Why contact child services?"

"You know Leonora; she wouldn't tell me. They didn't meet face-to-face, e-mails and phone calls only. That's all Mitchell would agree to. He won't meet with anyone. From how he sounded, she suspected things were bad. If she's concerned, so am I."

"What could you do for him?"

She twisted a strand of shoulder-length hair around her finger so tight the tip of the finger turned blue. "I don't know, but he saved my life. I owe him."

Mara's expression softened. "Take heart. Maybe he'll come out of hiding, and you can meet him some day."

Drawing a tense breath, she continued. "I already know where he is. Leonora accidently on purpose wrote his contact information on a slip of paper and allowed it to fall into my purse. I have his phone number and a PO box."

Looking appalled, Mara straightened. "That's so out of character for Leonora, I don't know what to say."

"I pleaded with her. You know how persistent I can be. Leonora talks tough, but she's all heart. She's practical, too. I think she's as worried about Mitchell as I am, and she knows she can only do so much."

Mara shrugged. "Where is he? Beverly Hills?"

"Los Lobos, the Black Hills. I checked Google Earth. The place barely exists. It's a whole lot of rural nothing. I've been calling the number. Believe it or not, it's a place called Gee's Bar."

A smirk crossed her mom's face. "I believe it."

"Mitchell won't take the call. The owner of Gee's Bar is supposedly giving him my messages."

"Honey, I would leave him alone. Stop calling."

"I can't. If I wait, he might move on. I could lose my only chance to thank him in person."

"Granted it was a huge ordeal, but you only saw Mitchell once. Do you think you might be idealizing matters?"

"Do you think I haven't had this exact conversation with my therapists a thousand times?" Raising her hands to her ears, she froze. "I'm sorry to snap. I didn't mean to. Why doesn't anyone seem to understand I need closure? I want to see with my own eyes that Wail'n Waya is a flesh-and-blood man, not a demigod, supernatural force of nature. I'm doing better. Now he's the one who's down for the count. If I can lift him up, even the tiniest bit, then I should do it."

"If he won't even talk on the phone, how are you going to contact him? E-mail? A letter?"

Her shoulders tensed. "I'm going to Los Lobos."

Mara sighed. "Who's going with you? Leonora?"

Fidgeting in the chair. "No. I told you, Mitchell refuses see anyone from his past."

"So?"

"So, I'm going to sneak up on him. I'm just going to show up. I don't have any other choice."

24

Shaking her head, Mara's gaze drifted up the wall. "Sweetie, that's a terrible idea."

"Just listen. It serves so many purposes." She pointed to her eyes. "I need to stand in front of Mitchell and make visual contact. If he's rude or turns out to be a regular guy, great! It will help me let him go all the easier. I can thank him and say good-bye. I'll be home for a late dinner."

"When is this scheduled to happen?"

"It's got to be today. I have to be back on campus Monday morning for the spring semester."

"What? Not today! Los Lobos is at least three and a half hours away. I can't drive you there. The contractor's coming to repair the porch."

"The hot-shit contractor who keeps smiling at you? Good for you, Mom!"

Mara blushed. "Don't try to distract me. This is serious. How are you planning to get there?"

"I'll drive myself."

"Alone?"

"I drive alone the same distance to Sioux Falls University."

"But the other way takes you into wilderness, toward a man you don't really know."

She glanced out the window to avoid the look of pain forming on her mother's face. "Mom, I can't explain it, but all my instincts are telling me I should do this. My conscience is howling at me to check in with Mitchell. Would Leonora give me his contact information if she had reservations about him?"

"I've always trusted Leonora's judgment, but...." Mara hesitated. "No matter what I say you're going to do this, aren't you? If I say no, you'll run to Los Lobos behind my back, right?"

"I don't want to worry you or lie. That's why I'm telling you where I'm going, who I'm meeting, and when I'll be back. I have everything in my purse. Phone, GPS, Glock, MACE. You have to allow me a little independence."

"Do I have let you do risky things?" She rubbed her eyes. "When did you plan on leaving?"

"Now. So I can return by tonight."

Knock, knock, knock. A heavy fist rapped on the door.

Mara rose and walked to the front door. "That's the contractor. He's early."

The moment she was alone, Christy plucked her phone from her pocket. With low expectations, she dialed Gee's Bar for the third time in two days.

On the fifth ring. "Hello," a male voice rumbled. "You've reached Gee's Bar. What do you want?"

"Is this Mr. Gee?"

"Just Gee," he growled.

"I'm Christine Killgaren, the journalist who wants to interview Mitchell Waya."

"I remember."

"Has Mr. Waya come to Gee's Bar yet? Have you given him my number?"

A rude snort. "He don't want to talk."

"So, you've spoken to him and told him about me?"

"Yep. He said the press can go...." An uneasy paused followed. "Make luck for themselves."

"Make luck?" She balked. "By any chance is he with you now?"

"He's shaking his head. So, I guess the answer's 'no.'"

"That's what I thought. Would you please tell Mr.

Waya I want to do a straightforward interview with him? No tricks or paparazzi. I'll give him a chance to tell his side of events."

A long pause followed before Gee returned to the line. "Too bad. You missed him. He just left."

"Later today, I'm driving past Los Lobos." She sounded too eager. "I'd like to stop for a short while. How do I find you?"

"I wouldn't do that, Miss," his tone was discouraging.

"Why?"

He grumbled, "Because spring thaw turned the dirt roads into slush."

"I can manage."

"Late-season snow coming."

"Then the slush would freeze wouldn't it? I've got chains."

"If you get snowed in, there's nowhere in town to stay."

"I'll think of somethi—"

"Miss Killgaren?" A younger, much grouchier male voice boomed through the phone. "Why can't you take a hint? There'll be no interview. I don't want to talk. Don't bother making the six-hour drive from Sioux Falls. You're wasting your time."

Her heart pounded. "Is this Mitchell Waya? I'm not in Sioux Falls. Today, I'm in Pierre. I can be in Los Lobos this afternoon. All I want is a few minutes of your time, please. It would mean a lot."

"I don't see the point."

"Meet with me and you might see the point."

"I'm sorry, Miss, I don't want to be rude...." He sounded contrite. "I don't do interviews anymore. Please stop calling."

The call ended. It took a moment for her to fully grasp that Mitchell had cut her off cold.

Internal alarm bells went off as the sad realization struck—she'd miscalculated and picked the wrong cover. Obviously, Mitchell didn't appreciate being cornered by the media he'd once mastered to advantage. Even the offer of sympathetic treatment and a chance to tell his side of events meant nothing. Her one opportunity to get close just blew up in her face. A sickening feeling she'd provoked his flight, and he might be packing his bags this minute, nagged. She had to reach Los Lobos before he fled. The clock ticked and the race started. She grabbed her monster tote bag containing everything she might need to survive a zombie apocalypse and ran downstairs.

"Mom!" she hollered, her voice echoing through the semi-restored clapboard home. "I'm heading out. I'll call from the road."

Mara rushed over to give her a hug. "I can't believe you're doing this."

"I have to."

"Be careful."

"I know, Mom. Try to relax. Reverend Simon is in prison now, and that's where he's going to—"

"Christy, I still panic every time you leave my sight," Mara whispered, so the contractor in the next room wouldn't overhear. "It's getting better, but I often wonder, what if we didn't fight that day? What if I'd reached you sooner? Reverend Simon never would have seen you at the damn convenience store and helped himself to my daughter. I still have nightmares about—"

Raising her palm. "Please don't. We can't change

the past. I love you. Remember we're not the guilty ones." It did hurt to think about it. Six years ago, when she was twelve, she and her mom had fought over some long-forgotten and petty thing. In a huff, she'd marched away from home and hid around the corner, near a convenience store. She sat near the main drag for a couple of hours, angry as a wet cat, listening to her mother call her name while not answering. As darkness fell, she considered returning home when a man driving an SUV asked if she'd seen a lost dog. She'd not seen any strays, and said so, but the man insisted on showing her a picture anyway. As she bent to look at the offered photograph, a rag soaked in chloroform clamped over her nose.

A hint of a brave smile warmed Mara's face. "Call whenever you stop, when you get there, and when you leave for home."

"I promise." She headed for the door.

Her mother had a point, and she understood her concerns, but sometimes it was too much. More than anything she wanted to be normal and do the things other people enjoyed. She didn't want to be the poor little girl from the Reverend Simon scandal anymore.

Mara gazed into her eyes. "Did you check your can of Mace? Have you charged your Taser?"

"Yep." She leaned close, delivering a quick peck on the cheek "Bye, Mom."

***

Mitchell loitered near the front door of Gee's Bar. The call from Miss Killgaren upset him. Los Lobos should his new sanctuary, a place so inaccessible and pointless no one would go out of their way to visit. So, how did the media find him? He'd been discreet.

Only one trusted soul outside the pack knew his whereabouts. Once Drew discovered this breach, all hell would break loose. Day one, he'd been warned pack exposure must be avoided at all cost. He considered loading his pickup with a few essentials and leaving town before an angry Enforcer threw him out.

He'd been as rude as he dared to the honey-voiced Miss Killgaren. With luck, he'd never hear from her again. Something about the woman's tone left him rattled. A soul-numbing, sense of emptiness opened inside. He needed to think and didn't want to stay at Gee's Bar to socialize with pack, and he sure as hell wasn't ready to go upstairs to his rented room to be alone.

For a moment, he considered heading over to Galveston's Gym to pummel his tensions away on the punching bag. A fellow MMA fighter, Ravage Galveston had slipped into the role of confidant-mentor with ease. During his first days back in the gym, even light training caused searing pain. But Ravage had challenged him and pushed him through those first crucial workouts. His strength and balance improved every day. Using the cane became optional. His injuries, which would have shattered a human life, merely slowed the Wolf in him. In the past month, he'd put on so much muscle Ravage predicted he'd make a full recovery by summer.

Gee stacked beer mugs behind the bar.

Mitchell took cautious steps toward the bar without leaning on the cane. Though his legs were strong, his knees were still tricky. He stopped in front of his hulking friend. "Gee, have you told Drew about Miss Killgaren?"

Gee thrust out his lower lip. "No, I was waiting to see how you handled it."

"I swear to God, I don't know how she found me."

He polished a mug with a cloth. "She found you. It doesn't matter how. I doubt she'll make it all the way out here, but if she does, we have a problem."

"I just settled in. I don't want problems."

Gee grunted. "Pack privacy comes first, my friend, and right now, you're high-profile. Unless you want to piss Ryker off and spend a few more months in traction, I'd volunteer to hit the road now."

"But then wouldn't Miss Killgaren hang around Los Lobos, looking for me and asking questions and possibly filming town? Think about it. Bad could get much worse. I do know something about the media. If you blow them off, it goes sour fast. They make up their own story. But if you throw them a bone, it's possible to take control of the situation."

Wagging a thick finger, Gee frowned. "We don't need a snoopy interviewer here."

"I'm not saying invite her, but if she shows up, we have to be ready. Warn everyone before they walk into Gee's Bar. Maybe I can distract her? Drive her out of town? Set a false trail and say I'm moving out of state, give her a fake address to chase."

"Sounds like a fuckup in the making."

"No." He tapped his cane. "Acting furtive and insisting no one can be filmed or talk to the media under pain of death is what rouses suspicion. If we're not careful, I'll become a footnote to the bigger story of the paranoid mountain town of Los Lobos. Trust me, that's not what you want. I say play it down. I'll give her a weak story and bore her to tears. Then we get rid of her as fast as we can before she sees or hears something damning."

Gee appeared to consider the plan. His heavy head slumped to his shoulders. "Nope. I don't like it. It's a shit pie of an idea with trouble baked into the crust."

"What? That's all I've got!"

With an impatient swish of his big hand, Gee mumbled, "Go."

"You mean leave the pack?"

"I meant take a run. Go off by yourself for a while. Let me handle this. Stay away until nightfall. By then, Miss Killgaren will have moved on."

"Bear knows best." Wanting to stay, he forced himself to walk to the edge of town. When he reached the tree line, he limped into the woods and stripped his clothes away. He left everything in a neat pile with the cane set atop the stack. Cold air prickled his bare skin. Glancing at his torso, he noted the many scars crisscrossing his body were fading fast. He shifted to wolf form then ran into the hills. The exhilarating sensation of blood pumping through his body always thrilled his senses. Though his bones were still healing, balance on four legs made movement easier, almost graceful.

He hoped Miss Killgaren would go away and allow him to live in peace with the pack. The town of Los Lobos had experienced a major change. Once a place of oppression, it had evolved into a shifter's paradise. In a heroic deed, the new Alpha, Drew Tao, killed the old tyrant Magnum Tao. With Magnum gone, the pack had flourished. For the first time in a generation, a steady trickle of diaspora like himself returned. Something his outcast parents could only have dreamed of.

Running to near exhaustion, a dreary afternoon turned to evening. A northern storm blew in, halting the first signs of spring. With an aching hind leg, he trotted toward town and located his snow-dusted pile of clothing beside a tree. After dressing, he returned to Gee's Bar. Being indoors again assaulted his senses. It took a moment to adjust. The explosive *clack* of a pool cue striking a ball deafened. People talked, laughed, and shouted above loud music. The warm scent of food hot from the grill made his stomach growl.

His cousin Rio hailed him from a booth. "Mitch!" Rio held his hand out, waiting for him to give it a friendly slap.

Sitting on the opposite side of the booth, Rio's wife, Sela looked radiant and very pregnant. She offered a parade queen wave. "Hi, Mitchell." Pointing to a heaped plate of onion rings, her eyes sparkled. "I made Rio drive me into town. I woke up from a nap with a hellacious craving for Gee's onion rings. I ordered way too much. Would you like a few?"

His stomach made an embarrassing grumble. "Thanks anyway. I'm going to order my own food."

Sela scooted across the seat to make room. "Sit with us."

Mitchell remembered he needed to check in with Gee. "Another time."

Rio nodded. "I understand. Visit us more often, okay? Promise me you won't turn into a lone wolf."

"I'll come by the cabin soon to fix those kitchen cabinets."

"Don't wait too long." Rio grinned. "We got a baby on the way. We won't want noise and sawdust after the little one arrives."

Sela rolled her eyes. "Five more weeks. I am so ready to sleep on my stomach again."

Mitchell smiled at Sela. She smiled back, looking like an angel. "Rio, you bastard, how'd you get so lucky?" A little stab of envy pricked his heart. "I'll let you get back to your onion rings."

Cautious of his knee, he turned and walked away. Rio made a good point, he did need more social contact than he'd been getting. Hungry and exhausted, he approached the counter, leaning hard on the cane.

With his back turned to the bar, Gee fussed with the glassware. From this angle, he looked like a hunchback behemoth protecting a hoard of beer steins.

"Gee!" he shouted above Steppenwolf's "Magic Carpet Ride."

Wearing a tense expression, Gee faced Mitchell and made a subtle slashing motion across his throat with his finger.

"Judging by your weird behavior, I take it things didn't go well with Miss *Kill-Garden*, or whatever her name is? I feel sick about this. Tell Drew I'll pack and be gone by morning."

Gee shook his head.

Mitchell leaned over the bar. "What am I missing? Is something wrong?" He glanced toward the poolroom, seeing only the usual Saturday night pack chaos. "I'm starving. Tell you what, I'd kill for a steak, but I'll settle for a burger."

"I'll buy you a steak." A smoky female voice straight out of a luxury car commercial, floated over his shoulder.

If he'd been in wolf-form, his hackles would have raised—high. *The lady on the phone!* He'd returned to Gee's Bar too soon and got busted. Glancing behind, he froze and stared in astonishment. The owner of the confident femme-fatal voice was a pretty, but down-to-earth-looking girl in her late teens. Her voice and petite body were a total mismatch. Judging by her demeanor on the phone, he'd pegged her as a worldly woman in her thirties, the type who wore heavy makeup and a jewel-toned power-suit. Instead, she dressed in casual denim and boots with so many rumpled layers of T-shirts and cardigans she looked like a hobo. Large hazel eyes beneath straight dark brows were her most outstanding features. The confidence of her direct gaze parried with a shy smile. For some inexplicable reason, he couldn't breathe.

"Mitchell, meet Miss Killgaren." Gee stood with his fists anchored to his hips. "She's been here for hours, sitting in the corner. Waiting."

"Hello, Mr. Waya. I won't bother with the formality of a handshake." Miss Killgaren glanced at the cane. "I definitely got the vibe I'm not welcome, so I'll do everyone a favor and make this quick. I'd like to ask you a few questions, and then I'll leave you in peace."

He glanced at Gee.

Gee offered a faint nod.

"Okay, but let's keep it brief." He hoped he sounded more relaxed than he felt. His senses reeled and body tensed, the same way he felt before a match.

She pointed to the corner. "That's the table I'm seated at."

He allowed her to lead. "You have to have better things to do on a Saturday than sit in a place like this. Why are you here?"

Looking over her shoulder with wide, innocent eyes. "You've been of interest to me for years."

"You don't look like the usual media contact. What's this about?"

The slight crooked line of her mouth lent the impression she smiled and frowned at the same moment, and left him intrigued. He couldn't figure out her intentions. Traveling the fight circuit, he'd grown accustomed to, even expected, women to offer themselves. With detached coolness, he accepted the boon or sent them away, knowing they weren't really interested in him. They wanted the thrill of seducing a modern-day gladiator and sharing a taste of danger.

But not her. He sensed that wasn't her objective. The encounter felt odd. As he moved closer, he noticed Miss Killgaren's clean, natural scent did a number on him. Human women usually didn't provoke such an immediate visceral reaction. She set him on fire, and she wasn't even trying to flirt. On top of that, she didn't appear to be offering him anything but a vague sense of confrontation.

A soft expression lit her face. "I'm a fan."

His chest tightened. Dizzy and nervous, he didn't feel right and wondered if shifting and running around all day in the cold might be the culprit for the odd sensations. "We can talk, but I have to eat first."

"Me, too. I drank about a dozen cups of coffee instead of a real lunch today." She extended a trembling hand as proof of the jitters. "I'm ready to order some food."

She pointed at Gee. "Is he always so sarcastic?"

Mitchell nodded. "Always."

"And you put up with it?"

He couldn't stop staring at the delicate lines of her face. "I've got nowhere else to go."

A crooked grin crossed her lips. "Well, you just answered my first question, which was, why would a man who's lived the fast-track international lifestyle hide in Los Lobos? Seriously, there's not much here."

"The only answer I can give you is it's quiet, but I'm leaving here."

"For where?"

"Someplace quieter." Inspired to be a gentleman, he pulled out a chair and waited for her to sit. "By the way, Gee's Bar isn't a steak type of place. I hope you won't be disappointed with a burger and fries."

"A burger would be fine."

"Gee!" he shouted over his shoulder. "Two cheeseburgers and fries."

"No cheese on mine," she added. "I'll pay. I appreciate you taking the time to sit down with me."

He shook his head. "Gee will put cheese on it anyway. In his mind, a hamburger comes with cheese. I've tried asking him to leave the cheese off mine, but he won't do it. He's an eccentric. I used to peel it away, now I just eat it."

"Okay."

"The burgers are on me. I've got a tab here, and I rent a room upstairs."

"Here?" She appeared scandalized. "You live above a bar? I figured you owned a trophy home somewhere nearby."

Settling into his chair. "Nope."

"This place looks rowdy. It must be hard to sleep."

How could he explain the *clack* of pool cues and blaring music filtering through the floorboards were pleasant alternatives to the angry voice in his head telling him he was a worthless jerk. "I don't mind."

Drumming her fingertips on the table, she glanced around. "So, the Tex Wilkins story is true? You really are broke?"

"Disappointed? You sure don't look like a gold digger."

She didn't skip a beat. A spark of compassion shone in her eyes. "You deserve better."

Her words sounded convincing as if she did care. He took a long look at her. Even a half-dozen layers of frumpy clothes didn't obliterate a graceful frame and hint of soft curves. Tons of wild auburn hair tumbled in waves around her face. Her lush lips sent conflicting messages. A new terror entered his thoughts. He half feared she might be one of the women he'd hooked up with on the circuit and long forgotten, or didn't recognize minus the heavy glamor makeup. He hoped to God he'd never messed with anyone this young. "Have we met?"

She seemed anxious, almost breathless. Her lips parted. "Once."

Panic set in. "I am so sorry if I did or said anything to hurt your feelings or mislead you. During a chunk of my life, everything moved so fast it became a blur. I'm not proud of my promiscuous behavior, but I can't say I regret it either. If I—"

Her jaw dropped. "What are you talking about?"

He gulped. "Have we...the two of us...you know?"

Her cheeks flushed. "No! Absolutely not."

"That's a relief. I'd hate to forget someone like you."

Turning her face, she stared at the wall. "I made a big mistake approaching you this way."

He threw his hands in the air. "I told you not to come. Don't pretend to be shocked. I thought you wanted a where-is-he-now interview. The more horrid stuff dug up about me the better, am I right?"

A look of indignity flashed in her eyes. After fishing her hand into her tote bag, she retrieved a smartphone and toyed with the coral case. "I didn't come all the way here to dig up more dirt. You already have enough out there."

That stung. "For sure there's enough bad news connected to my name. What do you want to hear? I thought you were some journalist from a television station, hoping to trap me in a gotcha moment when you announced something lurid like Tex Wilkins had been found strangled by a rope with my name on it. Tex deserves it, but just for the record, I'd never lay a hand on the sneaky bastard. I don't give a shit about the money. He can keep it and rot in hell." Narrowing his gaze. "You do look familiar. What's going on? You're not a journalist. You're just a kid."

"I am a student of journalism at Sioux Falls University."

"Jeeze," he huffed. "I think we're finished."

"Wait!" Her face became somber. "Just a couple more questions and I'll go."

"What's the point?"

She appeared agitated, fidgeting with the phone case, picking at it with a manicured fingernail. "You say you don't care about the money, but you sound, and look, pretty freaking angry when you talk about it."

"Working the circuit ain't for wimps. It's a hard

way to earn money. You have to push yourself to do things you don't want to do."

"Like punish someone in the cage more than you'd ever choose to?"

"Something like that." Most of the time, he took more punishment than necessary. Tex had a strategy to follow. It wasn't enough to just win. Tex wanted what he called "controlled decimation," but it had to be done a certain way. To keep the audience's interest, they needed to be tricked into believing his opponent stood a chance. Tex's strategy built on the pretense the match might not go his way by prolonging it. He didn't mind taking his time. The Wolf in him guaranteed minimal risk of exhaustion or injury. Plus, when he fought, he felt fully alive.

With brows level, her expression appeared frank. "You suffered a couple close calls in the ring but no losses. What do you credit your success to?"

"I rode out a lucky streak." In his weight class, he didn't have an equal. There were a lot of big guys on the cage circuit, but they didn't have his speed. There were a lot of fast fighters, but they didn't have his focus. On demand, he could turn on the juice and connect with the force of a wrecking ball and then just vaporize. "For a while, Tex made us rich."

"You mean Tex made himself richer. From my understanding, he'd made his fortune long before he ever signed you."

"Wrong." He knew an obnoxious shit-eating grin just hijacked his face, but it couldn't be helped. "When Tex signed me, he was dead broke with repo men for lawn ornaments and a Mexican cartel making death threats. He needed a winner in his pocket, bad. The dude burned through money. My fondest consolation is Tex didn't learn a thing. In no time, he'll spend all he stole from me and be back in debt. I'm going to sit back and enjoy watching Queen Karma cut him to shreds."

"Hold on a moment!" She scrolled downward on her phone and clicked. "I want to show you something that you just did."

"What the hell!" He balked. "Were you filming me without my permission? Give me that!"

Watching the screen, she continued to scroll. "Calm down. I'll let you delete it. Ah, there it is." She clicked on a still and handed the phone to him. "I've seen the look before. Hit Play. Watch what happens to your eyes when you say 'Queen Karma.'"

She leaped from the chair and stood at his side, looking over his shoulder at the screen. "See?" She sounded delighted. "Beautiful brown eyes. Nothing unusual. You do look peeved, and then *Bam!* The pupils detonate and flash amber like a flare. I saw it firsthand. Nothing in this room changed. The flash came from you."

"So?" He deleted the video, taking heart that she couldn't know anything concrete. Even Tex's allegations were vague. He'd been so careful about never shifting on the circuit. For over three years, he'd lived in complete denial. Always holding back and remaining in control. Never revealing his true self to anyone or allowing the Wolf within to run loose. What she hinted at could be dangerous and put the whole pack at risk. With the welfare of others in mind, Ryker—their Enforcer—would make him disappear.

"See?" Standing behind him with her hand placed on his shoulder, she leaned so close her warm breath bathed his cheek. Reaching over him, she clicked onto a photo gallery and scrolled. "There you are at Emperor's Palace."

He stared the photo of himself kneeling over his doomed opponent with his fist raised, a millisecond away from delivering the life-changing blow. His eyes blazed amber. Covering the screen with his palm, he shoved it away. "Delete this crap. I don't want to look at that."

"Because it's painful, or because you feel exposed?"

"It's an ugly moment. I'm not proud of it."

"Did Tex know about the avenging angel?"

He shuddered. "I don't know what you're talking about."

"Tex figured out you were different, didn't he? How could he miss the signs? Did he threaten you with blackmail? Mitchell, you're not like the rest of us, are you? For example, you heal so fast. No injuries in the ring. Your car accident put you through the blender. You should be dead, but instead I overheard one of your friends boasting you can punch a speed bag for three hours a day. Who does that straight out of traction?"

"Who told you?"

"Some guy named Ravage."

"Damn him." Hell couldn't be mad at Ravage; he counted the man a true friend. But the boast left him with some explaining to do. "Pin it on good genes or call it good luck. What's your point?"

"My point is I think I know a little secret about you."

Dreading exposure and the imminent flight, a gruff grunt crossed his lips. "What?"

Interrupting, Gee ambled to the table and set a heaped plate in front of her. "Here you are Miss Killgaren, Gee's Bar's best. Burger and fries with no cheese. Can I get you anything else?"

A hopeful grin crossed her lips. "Ranch dressing for my fries?"

Gee shook his head. "No ranch dressing. How about some pickle juice to dip your fries in? That's all we got."

Wrinkling her nose. "No, thanks. Ketchup will be fine."

Thrusting his lower lip out. "Why does everyone ask for ranch dressing these days? Am I missing a trend?" He set a plate in front of him. "Here you go Mitch. Cheeseburger and fries the way you like it." He turned and lumbered off.

He called after. "Gee, you didn't even ask if I wanted pickle juice."

Sounding grumpy. "I didn't ask because I know you don't." Gee returned to the table with the ketchup. "Miss, it's a Saturday night. We'll soon be serving alcohol in this section. I'm going to have to see ID proving you're over twenty-one, or ask you to leave."

With a gentle bite, she worried her bottom lip. "I'm eighteen."

"I'm sorry, but when you finish your food, you'll have to go." Gee glanced at his watch. "You've got ten minutes."

Mitchell rose from his seat. "Excuse me, Miss Killgaren. I'll be right back." He followed Gee and confronted him near the bar. "What the fuck, Gee? You allowed Ravage to speak to her?"

"I couldn't stop him. Ravage walked in here,

wearing his workout sweats, and Miss Killgaren approached him. She probably thought he was you. You know Ravage. He didn't say much."

"She just said she knew a secret about me. How ominous is that? I'm not going to force her to gulp her food down and leave before I know exactly what she's talking about. I'm going to need to do a little damage control here. Let's find out what she knows and what she plans to do with that knowledge before we turn her loose."

Gee's nostrils flared. "Yeah, I see your point, but make your investigation quick. Look around, amigo. The place is packed with 'pack.' Everyone is in town, socializing and drinking. It's just a matter of when some poor fool gets tipsy, shifts, and does a little *Dances with Wolves* routine on top of a pool table. That little girl you're breaking bread with is an outsider holding a camera phone. Add two and two, dude? It equals disaster!" He shoved a couple take-out containers into Mitchell's hands. "If you're wise, you'll think of a way to get her out of here before she sees something she shouldn't. The sooner, the better, because the new storm is dumping snow on the ground like a son of a bitch."

"I'll lead her off the main floor." He grabbed the take-out containers. "Someday, I'm going to find out why a fucking bear is in charge of a wolf pack's private business."

Gee grinned. "It's a fascinating story, quite heroic if I say so myself. Now shove off and encourage your pretty friend to leave ASAP."

Mitchell returned to the table. Miss Killgaren looked pensive as her hand hovered over her fries. Picking one up in her delicate fingers, she swirled it in a puddle of ketchup and bit. Glancing at the take-out containers, she frowned. "Is that a hint?" She pushed her plate away. "This was a bad idea. I did this all wrong."

She appeared angry, which made him feel worse. "You were starting to tell me something when Gee interrupted. You implied you knew a secret about me."

Planting her palm on her forehead, she sighed. "I wish I hadn't come here. I can see it's causing problems."

"I told you not to. I'll bet it's been a real disappointment to meet a washed-up cage fighter."

A harsh laugh burst passed her lips. "I'm not disappointed in you. This is so much harder than I thought it would be. It's stirring up a lot of weird feelings. To be honest, I didn't even come here today to interview you." She reached into her tote and pulled out a knit cap

"Then what is this about? Why did you come?"

Tucking her voluminous hair under a plain gray cap, she stood and donned a shapeless down coat. "I wanted to look you in the eye and say 'thank you and good-bye.'"

Something in his memory clicked. With his thoughts racing, he froze. He knew her! His lips parted, but the words stuck.

"So, thank you, Mitchell. I'll never forget you."

Looking her over, he didn't know where to focus. She'd been transformed. "Oh God!" His brain melted down while his heart did a happy dance. He'd always wondered what happened to the kid. She stood in front of him a beautiful, petulant woman. Before she could pull away, he grasped her wrist. "Christy?"

Chapter Three

C hristy marveled at the instant change in Mitchell's expression. A moment ago, he'd appeared so cynical. Now, he looked at her with a sparkling, indefinable something.

The grip on her wrist eased, and his fingers glided between hers and held her hand in a warm embrace. "I would never have recognized you. The face. The voice. Everything. Why didn't you say who you were right away?"

"I meant to, and then I got nervous."

"I thought about you all the time. When I read the details in the paper, it made me sick. I wished I killed those guys when I had the chance." He stared at her. "Looking at you now, I would never have guessed you were Child X from the Reverend Simon trial."

"Leonora invested so much trouble and time protecting my identity from the press. She made sure my court dates with the judge were private. No photos of me were taken. With subtle expertise, all of my requests to contact you were deflected."

"This was your secret?" His voice cracked with tender emotion. "You wanted to contact me? Christy, Leonora said it would be best if I stayed away. I didn't even know your last name."

"Leonora did a great job of shielding me. My mother's maiden name is Killgaren. I use it now. After the Reverend Simon trial ended, I almost lived a normal, if not an overprotected, childhood."

He pulled her toward the chair and motioned for her to sit. "Why did you lie? Did you think I wouldn't want to talk to you?"

"Leonora told me—"

Gee approached. "This section's now closed to anyone under twenty-one. Better use those take-out containers and call it a night."

Mitchell looked impatient. "Gee, give us a minute, okay?"

With a sour grunt and heavy footsteps, the bearlike man returned to the bar.

Mitchell squeezed Christy's hand. "I'm not letting you get away this time. I'll find a quiet place where we can talk."

Her head spun. Once again, Mitchell became the pillar of reassurance she couldn't get close enough to. He looked at her with loving concern. In a heartbeat, it all flooded back. The terror. The pain. Pure desperation. Then out of the shadows, salvation. A kind voice with a plan. An avenging angel whose earthly powers were unmatched—Mitchell.

Breaking free of his gentle grip, she picked up her plate and slid its contents into one of the containers. "Is there somewhere else in Los Lobos we could go? A coffee shop? Another diner?"

He laughed. "You saw the main drag. This is it."

"I'd ask again, why Los Lobos? But I get the impression I wouldn't hear the truth."

He glanced down at his boots, then up at her. A bashful expression colored his face. "We could go upstairs to my room-m-m," he stuttered. "It's comfortable. I promise it won't get weird."

Swallowing hard. "Okay." After all, she came here for him. In her mind, Mitchell earned extra points for figuring out her identity on his own and expressing genuine joy. It provided mild proof some bond between them existed. Now, she needed to work up the nerve to tell him all he meant to her and then dart into oblivion before she made a colossal fool of herself. "Don't forget your burger."

Ignoring the container, he picked up his plate and plopped her take-out container on top of his food. "Follow me."

"You just smashed your burger."

"It will be fine."

She stepped aside, so he could lead the way. With a slow but steady stride, he walked without leaning on his cane. He chose a roundabout path that circled the crowded bar, cut across the poolroom, past a storage pantry, and finally, up a back staircase.

"What do people who live here do for work?"

Glancing over his shoulder, he trudged up the stairs. "Lots of things. Aside from the local businesses, there are teachers, nurses, park rangers, and of course a sheriff. We even have a documentary filmmaker. At the moment, I'm one of the few that doesn't have an official job. I do odds and ends for Gee, but most of the time, we just get on each other's nerves." He laughed.

"This town's dainty digital footprint is

suspicious. When I Googled it, not much came up, yet it's a pretty rockin' place on a Saturday night. With my history, I'm sure you know why anomalies like this make me nervous. For years, Reverend Simon ran his own private compound, kidnapping the occasional girl to reward a follower. Would you care to tell me why Los Lobos is so secretive?"

"Are we secretive?" He slanted a sideways look at her. "You found us easily enough." They came to a rustic pine door. Mitchell leaned the cane against the wall, turned the knob, and pushed the door open.

"No key?"

"No need." Balancing the food in one hand, he stood in the doorway, allowing her to pass.

She entered the spacious cabin-like room. The steep, exposed-beam ceiling and single small window suggested the room had once been an attic. Woven Native American rugs hung against the knotty pine walls like fine tapestry, providing the only bursts of color to a shades-of-brown decor. The furnishings were sparse and included a well-used reclining chair, a tiny kitchenette with a hot plate set atop a mini fridge, and a large trundle bed shoved into a corner.

Looking around the room, she brushed her fingers against a stack of quilts. "Why is the bed set under the lowest part of the ceiling? You're so tall. Aren't you afraid you'll jump up some night and smack your head?"

A sheepish smile curled his lips. "That's already happened. I didn't see it coming as clearly as you." He pointed to a floor vent. "I wanted to be close to the heater."

"Ah." Moving on to a row of shelves. "What's on the other side of the wall?"

"Gee's room."

"That's nice. So, you can fight just by tapping on the wall."

He laughed. "Gee snores like a bear."

"Maybe he says the same about you?" Feeling nervous as hell to finally be alone with Mitchell, she did her best to hide it. In his publicity photos, he looked aggressive, intimidating, and self-assured. At this moment, he looked shy. His thick black lashes were beautiful. Most of all he looked younger than expected. Despite a sprint in life's fast lane, his face still bore a hint of innocence. "You're only twenty-two aren't you?"

He nodded. "Yes."

"Have you thought about what you're going to do next?"

He shrugged. "Fighting is all I've ever done."

"That's not completely true. I read somewhere you co-managed Hank's Hardware Gym."

"That's a generous exaggeration. Hank's a great guy. His heart is in the right place. In all honesty, janitor is a better job description."

After reading the magazine clipping so many times, she'd memorized it. "That's not what Hank said in the article. He said you helped him train the state championship high school wrestling team and taught the children's Tae Kwan Do program all by yourself. He mentioned after you went pro, the PR financially benefited the gym. Do you stay in touch with Hank?"

"As a favor to Hank, no," he grumbled. "He's doing good. I'm not the sort of guy he'd want hanging around a family business."

She walked toward the bed and sat on the edge of

the mattress. "You're not a monster or damaged goods. Believe me I know what I'm talking about."

With firm but gentle pressure, he placed a hand on her shoulder and motioned for her to move. "Don't sit there."

"Why?"

His face flushed. "I sleep there. Sit over here." He walked her toward the kitchenette, unfolding a small table and two jump seats from the wall. The table was closer in size to a large tray. He set the plate and take-out container down. "Have a seat."

She sat, relieved to discover the folding bench felt sturdier than it looked. Opening her take-out container she took hold of her burger. Her appetite returned, and she bit in with pleasure. "Yum. Gee is a damn good cook," she mumbled between bites. "Even cooled it's still great."

He bit into his. His eyes rolled heavenward. "I should have ordered two."

She realized she could probably eat two, also. "Can we order more?"

"Sure. I'll go downstairs in a few minutes and get more. It's best not to wait. On busy nights, if they run low on patties, Gee tries to force fried pickles on everyone."

An afternoon spent drinking acidic coffee made her stomach lurch at the mention of a pickle. "Eww. No."

"It doesn't sound good to me either."

For a minute, they ate in silence and watched each other across the table.

Mitchell shifted his long legs, bumping her with his knees. "I'm sorry. I'm used to eating alone."

"No problem." Even a light brush of physical

contact took her breath. She savored the luxury of looking at him. Dark, wavy hair tumbled around his face. She wondered when he'd cut it last. In this light, beneath the grainy scruff on his jaw, she noticed a slight dimple in his chin and a faded scar photoshopped out of most print promotions. The rough details made him even more attractive. As her gaze swept upward, she was startled to see his attention, laser focused on her. Their gazes met and locked as if captive under a mysterious force. For a heart-skipping moment, she couldn't look away.

Mitchell broke the gaze first. He rose from the bench and strolled over to the window. "Holy crap. Look at it coming down."

She rushed to his side. "Oh no!" High drifts of snow blanketed the street below. The business district looked like a white wilderness. A few heaped lumps lined the front of Gee's Bar. A sickening realization dawned. "My car is buried! How am I going to get out of here? Does Los Lobos have a snow plow?"

"We have a small plow, but it can't fight weather like this. I could dig your car out, but why? There's no way you'd make it to the highway."

"I reserved a hotel room in Rapid City."

His lip curled. "Cancel it. You'll never make it. Besides, I wouldn't even let you try."

"Does Los Lobos have a motel?"

"There's nothing. This room is the closest thing to an extended-stay motel Los Lobos has to offer."

"Christ. I can't even sleep in my car."

"You can sleep in my bed." The awkward words hung in the air. He ran a palm across his thick hair, smoothing a few strands from his brow. "I meant, you can sleep in my bed. I'll sleep on Gee's couch. Christy, I'd never assume...."

Fearless Mitchell looked as flustered as she felt. She wanted to kiss the determined line of his lips until they softened and he understood she'd cherish anything he willingly offered. God knew she'd always dreamed of having him as a friend or lover, preferably both. "I feel badly that I'm putting you out and causing problems. I'll bet you had other plans tonight."

"I didn't." A tense laugh escaped. "Welcome to my Saturday night! This is all I have to show for the last four years of my life. Everything I own is in this room. Okay, that's not completely true," he muttered. "I have a truck and a little money from a settlement Tex didn't know about." With strange intensity, he stared. "To be honest, your visit is the best thing to happen to me since the car accident last autumn. I mean that. The nightmare incident in the alleyway haunted me. I often wondered what happened, if you were okay. It's good to see you looking so...healthy."

"I thought of you often, also." Her hopes soared. "Can I ask you a personal question?"

Apprehension clouded his expression. "Go ahead."

"Do you have a girlfriend or someone who cares about you?"

"I've got no one. Maybe that's my problem."

"You don't have to sleep on Gee's couch. I can sleep in the chair."

His gaze softened. "It won't be comfortable."

Grazing her fingertips across a frosty windowpane. "It's better than becoming a human icicle out there."

"True." He sat at the table to eat the last of his burger. She joined him, finishing her food as well. Reaching toward a wooden bowl filled with red apples, he picked one up and polished it on his flannel sleeve. He dug into his pocket, retrieved a folding knife, and pulled out the blade.

The glitter of inlaid abalone shell and pearl caught her eye. "Is that a wolf on the handle?"

"Yes." With an open palm, he presented the beautifully crafted item for inspection. "This belonged to my dad. He carried it everywhere." He pressed the blade into the crisp apple skin, making it *crunch*, and sliced a sliver of fruit for her. "My dad would sit with me and my sister and divide candy bars, popsicles, everything with this blade. He said a man should always carry a knife and be ready to share."

Bringing the bit of sweet apple to her lips, she bit. She'd never known her father. "That's a nice saying."

"It's more than a saying. My dad shared everything." Pointing to a framed photograph on a near shelf. "That's my family."

She glanced at the photo, first noticing a slender teenage Mitchell and his look-alike father, standing on the bank of a lake. A young girl of about twelve or thirteen, wearing denim cutoffs and a smug smile, leaned her head against Mitchell's shoulder. "Did you get along with your sister? I always wished for a sister."

"Are teenage brothers and sisters supposed to get along? Isabelle gave me a lot of lip." A bittersweet smile crossed his face. "At fifteen, I started shaving. Issy made the most embarrassing comments about it in public, but I loved her. If she were alive, she'd be your age."

"I'm sorry."

"Me, too."

"We both have a lot of sad things in our past, don't we?"

He grunted. "Yep."

"It's hard to tell others about it, isn't it?"

He continued cutting and dividing the apple between them. "Uh-huh."

"It's like they want to know too much, or they don't want know about it at all. I've watched people shut down and turn away from me, once they find out who I am. It frightens them to know evil is loose in the world, and I'd been in direct contact with so much of it. Like the taint is contagious. They look at me like I'll never wash clean and always be damaged. I hate it. But the worst ones are too interested. You know the type, strangers who ask some gnarly-sick questions. I'm disturbed they'd be so fascinated. Sometimes I just want to explain—I'm more than my story. I don't want to dwell there. Being the victim or the movie of the week has zero appeal. "

His eyes glittered in the low light. "I know."

"Shame's a heavy thing to drag around, isn't it?"

Setting the knife down, he stood. "Come here."

She rose and stood in front of him. "I'm talking too much, aren't I?"

Wrapping his arms around her, he drew her close to his chest, enveloping her in a warm, flannel-clad hug. "You are not damaged. Please don't even say it."

For a luxurious moment, she allowed her hands to roam over the napped texture of his shirt, sensing the solid tension beneath. Brushing her face against his chest, she reveled in the full-blown feeling of safety and peace she'd been craving. Allowing another man so close would have been unthinkable, but Mitchell felt right. Pressing her ear to his chest, she listened to his heartbeat. "It feels strange to be here with you, talking."

He broke the embrace first. Pulling away, he grazed his fingertips across her cheek. The light touch lingered. "Do you want to watch TV?"

"Sure."

Picking up the remote control, he then clicked on a small flat screen fastened to the wall. The television lit. Tilting her head, it became obvious there was no angle to comfortably view from other than the bed.

"I've got satellite. I'm surprised we have a signal during a storm this heavy. It could go out at any time." Clicking up and down the channels, a show in black and white appeared.

"Stop." She stepped toward the screen. "This episode is one of the original *Twilight Zone's*. Did you ever watch these?"

"I never watched them, but I'll give it a try."

"We came in late. See those people looking confused in that clean, deserted town. They end up riding a train, traveling in a loop to nowhere. Just as they are getting suspicious something's fishy, the camera pulls back, and we see they're miniature models trapped on a toy train table, and a child is running their lives." She paused. "Oh. I just ruined the surprise, didn't I? Forget it."

He clicked to another channel. "How about a *Doctor Who* marathon?"

"I never watched *Doctor Who*. You'll have to

explain it to me or bring me up to speed."

Appearing scandalized, his lips parted. "You never watched *Doctor Who*? Everybody watches *Doctor Who*!"

She shrugged. "Not me. How many episodes have I missed?"

He slumped. "Um. The show's been on for more than half a century. Where do I start? There's a Time Lord. He's the Doctor. Although he looks human, he's an alien. But he loves humans and can't stay away from them. He's always trying to save somebody, and sometimes he gets killed."

Stepping closer, she gazed into his eyes. "Why do you like the show?"

He stared back. A mixed array of emotions flickered across his face. "It's a constant. I don't have many of those."

With his tousled hair and widened eyes, Mitchell looked like a big kid. The sight pierced her heart. For a moment, she wished she could cleanse the past for both of them and steal a taste of what any other carefree young man and woman might feel for each other. She always hoped someday she'd meet someone and the attraction would be so strong it would override all obstacles. Looking at Mitchell, the possibility he might be the one became real.

She couldn't resist doing what she'd been dying to do. Rising on tiptoe, she clasped her hands against the sides of his face and drew him into a kiss. The first touch was featherlight, barely more than a shared whisper of warm breath. He didn't pull away, his hand brushed hers, caressing her fingers. Encouraged by his sweet response, she grew bolder on the second pass. With a sweep of her tongue, she tasted the tart hint of apple on his lips.

"Christy...." he whispered. "What are you doing?"

Clasping her hands around his neck, she drew him near. For a fleeting moment, her mouth pressed to his, and she felt him relax. Her excitement built as she glided her knee between his. The tight denim of his jeans did little to mask the hard rise brushing her thigh. The instant reaction to her touch was like a match set to straw.

Tensing, he pulled away. "We should stop."

Embarrassed, she fought back a wave of devastation. "I'm so sorry. I thought I sensed something between us."

"You did." The expression on his face was flustered and his voice hoarse.

"Why stop? Please don't say you still think of me as a kid. You of all people should know what it's like to grow up too fast. Is it me? Maybe I'm not your type?"

"That's not it." He moved toward the window and stared out. "You're a beautiful woman. I love what I see."

Joining him at the window, she watched the snow flurries swirl. She waited in silence for Mitchell to speak, as long moments passed.

He glanced sideways at her. "I can't treat you casually. You deserve better. There's no way I could kiss you a second longer and still be able to stop. I don't trust myself. We just met and this feels too good, too comfortable."

She reached for his hand, but he drew it away and thrust it inside a pocket. "I agree, but why do you need to stop? We're both consenting adults. I want you to know, this is not my usual behavior."

In a heartbeat, he appeared to collapse into someone smaller, more fragile. Even his voice softened. "There are things about me that make me different in a way that would be difficult to accept."

Inching closer, her arm brushed his. "Mitchell, you can tell me anything. I'll listen with an open mind."

His reflection on the dark pane looked somber. "I can't tell you because it's not my secret to share."

She battled the desire to place a hand on his shoulder and comfort him. "Can you share any of the secret?"

"I shouldn't. The responsibility of knowing would be unfair to you. After what you've been through, you deserve something uncomplicated and normal. You're way too young to get pulled into the stuff I'm carrying around."

"Have you talked to anyone about this?"

"Gee is the closest thing Los Lobos has got to a confession box. Even he can only take so much. One day, I tried to tell him about Robert Meadows—"

"Who is Robert Meadows?"

"His name on the MMA circuit is 'Slam Cyclone.' You heard about it. He's the man I made into a quadriplegic. I didn't know he was married with two young daughters. To be honest, I didn't care. Until I hurt him so bad he'll never make love to his wife again or hold his children in his arms. I did that to him. The worst part is I can't think of a justifiable argument why. It certainly didn't make me proud. Tex split with the purse, so there was no profit. Every day I imagine Robert in his bed, hating me. For reasons I won't explain, I healed from a car accident that should have killed me or, at the least, left me in the same condition as Robert. Justice might have been served. Instead, I healed. I'll be back to one hundred percent in no time. I'm almost ashamed of it."

She leaned against the wall and felt the chill of the storm leak through. "Would you say the car accident might have been a self-inflicted punishment for what happened to Robert?"

"Maybe."

"Have you considered your miraculous healing might be a gift? Maybe you're strong and whole because you're not finished doing good deeds?"

He looked away. "Or bad. It's ironic telling you this. I'm built to fight. It came easy to me. Four years ago, what I did in the alleyway might be the purest thing I ever committed to in my life. Those men were hurting a kid and needed to be stopped. I felt no conflict in my heart or mind. The cage is a different story. Robert was just a guy like me but with more to lose."

She reached for his hand, and unlike earlier, he didn't recoil. "I don't often get credit for being able to cope with reality as well as I do. If you have something going on in your life that makes you feel alone or unable to share your true self, I am exactly the right person to talk to."

He looked into Christy's soft hazel eyes. Had any angel in heaven ever looked so compassionate? In so many ways, they were alike. He'd seen the world, and she'd seen the world's shadow. They were both too young to be so brittle. She appeared to have survived her hell with her heart wide open. Something he could only dream of. Even more enviable, she possessed wisdom beyond her years, wrapped in peaches-and-cream freshness. His scars showed on his body and attitude.

"Mitchell, you're not saying anything. Did I put you on the spot?"

"I'm thinking." A weird jittery sensation overtook him. His Wolf instincts shouted *She's perfect for you!* He wanted to hold her and nuzzle his face against her hair. Take her to his bed. Laugh with her, talk with her. Know she would be at his side, smiling when he woke in the morning. The sensations were new. Since he'd been orphaned, he'd persuaded himself "loner" was his natural state. Looking at her, he knew something inside shifted.

"May I give you a compliment?" With a bashful smile, she glanced down. "When I turned fifteen, I took Tae Kwon Do classes. My therapists thought learning some form of self-defense would be a good exercise in personal boundaries and help build my physical confidence. Let's just say I found it challenging. After struggling for months to improve the tiniest bit, I could appreciate your speed, skill, and weird ability to read your opponent's mind. You're supernatural."

She gave him *that* look. As if he were some great prize. God, he wished he weren't so scared to fall off the edge of the pedestal. At this stage of his non-career, it wouldn't be too far a drop. Poor Christy. He'd confessed one of his guiltiest acts, and she still thought him special. "I'm different in a way that most people wouldn't understand or like."

Grasping his hand, she then brought his fingers to her lips and gave them a gentle kiss. "Why do you look so worried? You don't want to talk about this, do you? Do you think you have to be perfect all the time just because another part of your life went sour? I don't think so."

Closing his eyes, he allowed his thoughts to float for a moment on the sound of her voice. She touched his heart in a strange way that soothed as much as excited. He wanted to believe she could accept him. With his chest tight, it got hard to breath. Unannounced, the Wolf in him desired a life mate and chose her. He tried to tamp the feelings down, but all his senses focused on Christy. To his despair, every detail felt right, even her scent. A fact his inner Wolf found confusing. The attraction to her connected with the force of a roundhouse punch. Things were moving too fast between them. For a second, he almost convinced himself it might be okay to tell her everything.

"You can trust me, Mitchell. I'd never judge you."

He wanted to shout, *I'm a goddamned Wolf!* But the communal secret could not be revealed. No one in the Black Hills pack would forgive him for deliberate exposure. If trouble came of it, Christy might inadvertently come to the Enforcer's attention. A violent fate she didn't deserve. Inviting this sweet-tempered woman into his bed only to face yet more personal danger and an uncertain future would be cruel.

Just as he worked up the nerve to march downstairs and beg Gee to sleep on his couch, a tree branch near his window became so laden with snow it cracked with a brutal snap. The limb fell to the ground with thundering *swoosh*. A moment later, the television screen flickered with gray flecks and emitted loud burst of static. The show disappeared, and a "service disruption" banner appeared.

Feeling agitated, he picked up the remote then clicked off the television. "Whoops. Lost signal. No more *Doctor Who*."

She shivered. "It's damn cold leaning against this wall."

"Sorry." He motioned for her to follow. In a gallant gesture, he reached for a quilt and wrapped it around her shoulders.

Standing near the bed, she clutched the quilt. "It's much warmer over here."

He sat on the mattress and patted a spot beside him. "Have a seat."

"I thought you didn't want me sitting on your bed."

"I lied." A tense laugh burst free of him.

With a sunny smile, she laughed, too. "Good. I just finished scolding myself for coming on too strong and making you uncomfortable."

"No need." Beneath the rumpled quilt, she looked lost. He folded the edge down so he could better see her face. "What shall we do now? Do you play cards?"

"I don't know any cards games."

"Tex taught me lots of card games to play on the road. Come to think of it, he cheated. Never mind."

Bundling the quilt closer, she swayed. "I don't need to be entertained."

She looked down, and a wing of glossy hair fell over her eye. He swept it aside.

"Why did you come to see me today? This meeting might have happened anytime in the past four years, or years in the future. Why today?"

Drawing a tense breath. "Wow, my turn in the hot seat."

"You don't have to answer."

"But I want to. It's important. I didn't contact you sooner because Leonora discouraged it. Besides you were traveling the world as Wail'n Waya with plenty of responsibilities and distractions...."

Distractions was the operative word. In his first days on the road, a beautiful blonde materialized at his hotel room door. Funny and sexy as hell, she tumbled effortlessly into his bed. They spent an amazing three-day weekend together, fulfilling every one of his as yet unjaded fantasies. She fawned over him and never left his side. He thought he'd fallen in love. But just as he braced to ask if she'd be willing to travel the circuit with him, he'd walked in on Tex counting a stack of hundred dollar bills into her open palm. She didn't even look surprised when he entered the room. Her only explanation? A quick peck on the cheek and a halfhearted, "I'm sorry. I thought you knew."

"I turned eighteen in December," Christy continued. "I'm an adult now. I didn't want to cause trouble. I figured I should contact you now before you did a bigger disappearing act and dropped off the map."

"I think I already know, but how did you find me?"

The line of her lips tensed. "I'd rather not say."

"I understand."

Shadows obscured her features. Only her eyes glistened in the dark. "I came here today because I needed to see you...again."

"Why?"

She twisted the hem of the quilt between anxious fingers. "It's personal. First, I wanted to thank you face-to-face for ending my nightmare. I saw you jog away the first time. You didn't have to come back, but you did," her voice trembled. "They were going to kill me."

"You don't have to thank me."

"I know I don't *have to*, but I need to. This is where I'm going to sound silly. Bear with me. I hope to God I don't make you cringe." She gulped a deep breath. "For the last four years, I've had this haunting, larger-than-life image of you in my mind. You can't deny you were my hero that night. Then the media blitz hit. I saw your face on products and the sports channels. It sort of got out of hand."

"And you're looking for reassurance I'm just some guy who fucked up?"

"I wouldn't say it that way. I needed to see you were human."

He winced, unable to own the claim.

"My childhood ended prematurely, but this is my fresh start as an adult. I want to be like everyone else. Do what they do. Finish college. Get a job. Find a boyfriend." Allowing the quilt to drop to her shoulders, she slid closer. "But I can't because once I turned eighteen, someone released my full name to the public. Now everyone on campus knows I'm 'that' little girl. The past comes up all the time. But the worst part is I can't go on a date or get excited about anyone because...." Her face collapsed.

He got nervous as hell.

"No one compares."

"Oh God. I have to stop you—"

"Wait. I came to Los Lobos, expecting to be

disappointed. I planned to sit down with you and talk, see the flaws, and get disillusioned. Then say a quick 'thank you and good-bye.' Cross my heart, I wanted to be free. Now, how am I going to move forward?"

"What do you mean?"

With skittish actions, she crossed and uncrossed her ankles. "You're a great guy. Instead of wishing I'd find someone else like you, I'd like to get to know you better."

His gut churned. They were headed toward disaster. The heroic thing to do would be to smother hope and allow her to move on. "Christy, I'm going to be honest with you. You should walk away. I'm not what you think. This would never work. I know this sounds like bullshit, but one day, you will thank me for telling you to move on."

"Can we stay in touch and be friends?"

"It's a bad idea."

She looked hurt. "I'll drop it."

"Christy, I meant—"

"It's okay. You listened and gave me a chance to say what I needed to say."

"I'm saying all the wrong things, aren't I?" He glanced toward the door. "I'm going to ask Gee if he can put me in his room tonight."

"No, don't do that. I'm the one who should leave."

"I'm not putting you out tonight. Besides, there's nowhere else to go."

"It's been a long day. I'm exhausted." She plopped down in the easy chair. "Throw me another quilt. I'll be asleep in ten minutes."

He rushed toward her and grasped her arm. "Get

up. I'll take the chair. You take the bed."

Her lips drew taut. "It's your bed."

He tugged a little harder. "Please, I'm offering."

The line of her mouth remained resolute. "I'm fine here."

Taking hold of her wrist, he coaxed her to rise. "The bed is more comfortable. I'll feel better."

Resisting his motions, she dug in like a badger. "I'll stay."

"Sitting so close to the window, you'll freeze. Don't be so stubborn." He leaned over, scooping her into his arms, quilt and all. After carrying her to the bed, he dropped her on the mattress.

Landing on her side, she looked indignant. "That wasn't fair." Rising on her elbow, she cast the quilt aside and bolted toward the chair.

"Oh no, you don't!" He rushed toward the chair and launched himself into it at the exact moment Christy became airborne and landed in his lap.

"Ouch!" She smacked down on him before sinking between his thighs.

His arms locked around her waist when she tried to wriggle away. "Are you okay?"

Heaving a deep breath. "Yes."

"Good." He longed to keep her on his lap but released her instead.

She walked over to the bed, threw herself down, and started laughing.

For no reason, he laughed, too.

"We must look foolish."

He laughed harder. "I'm sure we do."

Still laughing as she slipped her boots off. "You can have the damn chair."

"You can keep the damn bed." Snatching a quilt

for himself, he realized for the first time in a long while, he was happy.

Chapter Four

Climbing under the covers, Christy settled into Mitchell's bed. The red flannel sheets with snowmen printed on them looked too Christmasy for late March but felt cozy on such a stormy night. "Who's going to turn out the lights?"

"I will." Mitchell tossed the quilt aside. "I'm going to brush my teeth."

She bolted upright. "I need to brush, too."

"I've only got one toothbrush."

"I carry a small armory. Fortunately, I'm prepared to fight plaque as well. There's a mini in my purse."

Pointing toward the bathroom door. "Ladies first."

She entered the dark bathroom. "Where's the light switch?"

"Above your head. Pull the chain."

Flailing her hand at the air until a metallic link came to her hand, she gave it a tug. The single bulb glared. The tiny room was literally a plumbed closet with a sloped ceiling.

"It's not fancy," he called from the far side of the room.

Setting the tote bag on the sink, she hunted for the dental kit with its travel toothbrush and tiny tube of minty paste. "Fancy doesn't matter." She almost reminded him she'd spent months living with Reverend Simon in unplumbed cabins and earthen bunkers outfitted with foul latrines, but the past felt irrelevant.

She squeezed speckled blue toothpaste onto the baby-sized brush as she looked in the bathroom mirror. *Mitchell.* His name floated through her thoughts as she cleaned her teeth. What a puzzle he'd become. Open and childlike one moment, full of brooding secrets the next. For years she'd carried a certain picture in her mind of who he might be, a warrior, hero, avenging angel, and ultimately fallen angel. All those lofty descriptions applied, but she liked the complicated man who got bashful, said stupid stuff, or laughed like a kid even better.

She finished brushing her teeth then sat down to pee. After she washed her hands in cool water, she exited the bathroom.

Mitchell sat on the bed holding the remote. The glow of the television provided the sole light in the room. "Good news. The signal's back." After handing her the remote, he headed toward the bathroom. "Choose something. I'll watch whatever you like." The door shut behind him.

Clicking through a few channels, she came to the conclusion pickings were slim. Her gaze drifted toward a bookshelf filled with murder mysteries, well-worn philosophy tomes by Plato and Aristotle, and a wide selection of science fiction fantasy including H.G Wells and Jules Verne, which she loved, too. A stack of college-level math texts were within reach of the bed. She peeked inside one dog-eared book and saw the pages covered with inscrutable penciled equations.

Remembering to cancel the hotel room in Rapid City, she reached into her tote for her phone and clicked. Then for the fourth time today, she called her mother. Mara didn't pick up. The message went straight to voice mail. "Hi, Mom. I'm snowed in. I'm not even going to try to drive until the roads are plowed. I'm spending the night in Los Lobos. I've got a room with a lock on the door, and I feel completely safe." She winced a little at the last part. "I love you. I'll call in the morning."

The door opened. Mitchell emerged with damp hair combed away from his face. Bold cheekbones and a longish nose lent his face a breathtaking elegance. For a second, she simply stared.

He smiled, brightening the room. "Anything on TV?"

"Nothing." She motioned toward the bookshelf. "Have you read all those?"

He sat beside her on the bed, "Yep, a couple of them two or three times. I read a lot on the road. Would have gone nuts if I didn't."

Taking a chance, she offered an opinion. "You should go to college."

He stroked the light stubble on his chin. "The opportunity came and went. I feel too old."

"You're not! I promise. I see all ages in my classes."

"Really? Something to think about." Taking hold of the remote, he clicked a few channels. "Look!

Dumb and Dumber is on. You said there was nothing to watch. Shame on you."

"Uh!" She groaned. "*Dumb and Dumber* is always on."

Leaning back on his elbows, he settled his weight on the mattress. "You have to admit it's funny."

"It is." She felt encouraged he didn't feel the need to get up and move away from her.

The movie lumbered along. Mitchell beamed. She knew every line but found herself laughing anyway because he did. During a commercial break, she caught him looking at her.

"What?"

"I'm glad you came to see me today. It feels like something has come full circle."

"It does."

"So, you grew up and went to college. What else is going on in your life?"

Grabbing a strand of her hair, she twisted the ends. "A lot and not enough. I don't know how to answer."

"Do you have a boyfriend you hang out with?"

"No."

"Just no?" He pulled himself upright, clasping his hands in front. "You mean not at the moment or no one serious?"

Drawing her knees to her chest. "I mean not ever."

"Nobody? That surprises me."

"Does it? Think about it."

"What are you looking for in a boyfriend-d?" he stuttered.

"Hundred-percent trust and a sense of safety. Mention that to guys my age and watch them scatter like cockroaches fleeing a kitchen light."

"There's someone out there. For a different set of reasons, I'm in the same boat."

Biting her lip. "I used to dream about you."

His face flushed. "Oh, come on—"

"Wait, let me make my point. Before today, I carried the most vivid image in my mind of what you would be like in real life. Beneath the public face, I expected you to be aloof, a bit mean, but you're not. You're just a big innocent kid. Even I could teach you things."

He huffed. "I'm sure you're right."

Unfurling her legs, she crept closer on all fours. Stopping in front of him, she brushed the tip of her nose against his. "I would trust you to kiss me and stop if I asked you to."

For a moment, he looked scared. "You shouldn't trust me."

"I sense I can."

When he slid away, the mattress flexed under his weight. "Christy, I'm in a situation that might put you at risk. You don't want to be associated with.... I'm a...." His brow furrowed, mouth tensed.

"It's okay if you're not feeling it."

Eyes shining. "But I am. You don't understand."

Giving his hand a squeeze. "You don't have to say it."

His lashes dipped. "I haven't been with anyone since before my car accident months ago. I'm not even sure I can...."

"You're getting ahead of yourself. No pressure. Just a kiss. I would love it."

"I meant control myself," his voice dipped to low husky tones. "Christy, having you in my bed is way more temptation than I can handle."

"I think you can handle it." Straddling his thighs, she faced him. Her hands skimmed his flannel shirt, taking in the swooping topography of the solid chest beneath. She cupped the sides of his face. Her gaze locked with his. Mitchell's eyes widened, his pupils pooled black. She pressed a gentle kiss to one temple and then the other. "See how easy?"

"You seem fragile, and then you're so aggressive." The tempo of his breath quickened.

She pressed her lips against his. "I've already experience the bad. I refuse miss out on the good." Delivering a lingering second kiss, she brushed a strand of his hair from his brow. "Are we okay? Should I stop?"

He returned the lightest kiss. "I would never have guessed what a little she-wolf you are."

Gliding her lips across the rough grain of his cheek, she murmured, "Is 'she-wolf' a compliment?"

He clasped her in his arms, holding her close, his face in her hair. "Oh yes."

Mitchell battled the urge to topple Christy onto the mattress—something he knew absolutely should not happen. Not this time. He vowed to allow her to explore him in complete safety. Christy needed his tenderness. To build trust, he willingly became her prisoner.

Having Christy astride his lap tested his self-restraint like nothing he'd ever experienced. He'd never felt such a strong attraction. The lonely Wolf in him wanted to howl with joy over the discovery of a potential mate. Gently rubbing his face against her hair, he inhaled the fresh scent of her shampoo, but beneath the balsam notes lay so much more. Like a whiff of incense snaking on the breeze, the tang of female arousal and something mysterious teased his senses and left him with a hard cock and a pounding heart. It could have been a wishful delirium, but he thought he'd caught a faint scent of Wolf on Christy. With so many pack members near, he couldn't be sure.

Her kisses were soft and playful. She seemed fascinated by the swell of his bottom lip gliding, sucking and nipping it between her teeth until he melted. Parting his lips with the tip of her tongue, she teased him with slow sweeping strokes. The sensations she provoked drove him crazy.

He tangled his fingers in her hair and held her close as he kissed her mouth.

She reached for his collar. "May I unbutton your shirt?"

In her eyes, he saw a hint of mischief. "Yes."

Unfastening the top buttons, she pushed the plaid flannel aside to expose his chest. She skimmed her fingertips over every inch of revealed flesh, pausing to bring his nipple to a point then swirling her fingers in the thickest patch of hair in the center. "I always wondered what you'd feel like. Your hair is silky." Beaming she tugged her sweater off followed by a gauzy T-shirt until only a thin camisole remained that did little to cover her luscious curves. The clear outline of large plum nipples shone through. Taking his hand in hers, she brought it to her breast. The tips peaked. "It's cool in here. I want to lie skin to skin with you under the covers." She slid the camisole's strap from her shoulder. "Warm me up."

Unable to answer, he shook his head.

"Please."

"Christy, you're killing me."

"Speaking for myself, I could use a little pleasure and few more positive experiences in my life." She pressed her lips to his forehead. "Should I stop kissing you?"

His throat tensed. "We are way past kissing."

"I know." Rising, she climbed off his lap, unbuttoned her jeans, and wiggled them down her thighs. Her shapely legs and a pair of peach panties offered a visual feast to his lust-starved senses. "Well?" Her eyes sparkled. "Take something off."

His cock strained to be freed. They were at the point of no return. Once her bare skin touched, his, the Wolf within would burst to the surface, fangs bared, insecurities and all, wanting to make a claim. "I shouldn't."

Sliding the other strap from her shoulder. "I wish I could put you at ease and make you feel as safe as you make me feel."

"Christy, do you have any consensual experience?"

She climbed under the bed covers. "None."

"That's what I thought." Her words were a sobering bucket of ice water dumped on his lap. "Sweetheart, this is not a good idea."

"Are you afraid I'm not ready for this? I can assure you I am. In my mind, this is a rite of passage where I'm in control. Mitchell, you're my first choice and always have been."

He closed his eyes to block the alluring look on her face. She had no idea what she awakened in him.

Not only would he have a hard time controlling his fiercer passions, it would be almost impossible to avoid bonding. Sharing such an intimate level of pleasure, looking into her eyes, committing her scent to memory, would push him over the edge. After this, he'd dream, obsess, and even willingly die for her. If there were to be any hope of keeping her as a mate, many hurdles needed to be cleared. As a human, Christy's presence in the pack would have to be approved by Drew and Ryker. On pain of death, she would have to commit to pack secrecy. A mate bond was for life, and for all he knew, she wanted a weekend lover to break the ice on her adult sex life. "We just reconnected. I need to be one hundred percent sure before—"

"Mitchell, I'm scared that this is my only chance to be with you."

"Why do you say that?"

Drawing the sheet higher, she stretched onto her side. "You didn't want to be found this time. Next, you might disappear completely."

He brought her fingers to his lips and kissed them. "I wish I could say some magic words, but the truth is whatever happens between us can't be casual."

"I don't want casual. Are you afraid I'll hurt you?"

He swept a lock of hair from her cheek and leaned closer. "No, I'm afraid I might do something selfish that would get you hurt."

"Mitchell, hurt has already happened to me. Fear isn't going to run my life. I want to live by my choices. If you feel a fraction of what I'm feeling toward you, where's the harm?"

The Wolf in him wanted her so badly, he almost growled. He needed to take decisive action. "Do you have a condom in the giant tote bag?"

"No."

He'd guessed correctly. Squeezing her hand, he looked into her eyes. "I'm sorry, but neither do I." There was no way in hell he could explain why the Black Hills wolf-shifters were different from the human population. They didn't pass STDs, and female shifters had discrete fertile cycles. Only human lovers required precautions.

She looked crushed. "I never dreamed things would go this way."

"Don't worry." He drew her into his arms and rocked her against his chest. "Everything's perfect." Slipping beneath the covers, he pulled her beside him. "Put your head on my chest."

Wrapping her arms around him, she snuggled close. "Sorry I let things get so out of hand. I should have asked about a condom first."

"It's okay." He really wanted her, but even more, he wanted things between them to be right. His thoughts wandered toward how he would explain Christy's situation to Drew.

"I'm disappointed," she sighed.

"Welcome to the adult world of sex."

They both burst out laughing.

"I meant I'm disappointed in myself. I pressured you and put you on the spot."

He kissed her cheek. "No you didn't." Gazing out the window, he watched gusts of snow blowing sideways. The sight provided a little consolation. No one would blame him for refusing to turn a woman out on a stormy night. Christy felt wonderful pressed against him. Being so near a potential mate provided a level of temptation he'd never endured. No matter how heated the situation, the man had to remain in charge of the Wolf. That meant no penetration, no wolf-play, no mate bonding, no claim biting. In short, he must avoid the things his wolf soul craved. "I know how to make you feel good."

Christy stretched across the sheets. "Show me."

He glided on top of her, taking his weight on his elbows. Touching his lips to hers, he murmured, "All you have to do is relax."

The pulse beneath her ear enthralled him. He lingered on the warm skin, sensing the blood rush. Cupping her breasts, he pushed the camisole higher, baring smooth curves. The man and wolf within were excited to fevered pitch to see such beauty displayed on his crimson sheets. Her dark nipples stood in stark contrast to her fair complexion. Leaning down, he kissed her breasts. Circling a nipple with his tongue, he brought it to a glossy peak. The wet kiss lingered as he sucked the bud passed his lips. Her soft moan provided instant reward.

Lifting his face, he whispered, "I want to taste you."

Stroking his fingertips along the sides of her hips, he pulled her panties down her legs and tossed them aside. With a gentle embrace, he stroked her thighs and placed her ankle on his shoulder. He lowered his face between her legs and brushed a soft kiss against her mons. Her warm, musky scent set him ablaze. The instant realization struck, this was a really bad idea. The Wolf wanted to throw its head back in a victory howl. Were it not for the confinement of tight denim with steel buttons, he would have burst free. The first stroke of his tongue to slick flesh took him straight to the edge. He swirled the tip of his tongue against her hard little bud. She wriggled like crazy, making sweet sounds. Christy's molten-hot response to his touch made his head spin. Taking his time, he sought deeper intimacy with each caress.

She wrapped her thighs around the sides of his face and rocked. In a string of broken whispers, she begged for more. Twice he brought her to the edge and twice he pulled back. Soon, her breathing sped and her light touch became a grasp. Tangling her fingers in his hair, she held him captive against her as a telltale cry of abandon broke free. Arching against the mattress, she trembled. "Mitchell." His name was uttered as a breathy moan. In the next moment, she relaxed onto the sheets, eyes closed.

His cock pressed hard against his jeans. Her enticing scent hung between them. He faced danger now. The slightest caress, a gliding mouth against his skin would summon the Wolf and it would all be over. There would be no restoring reason.

"What about you?" She stroked a slender finger along his thigh. "I can't leave a man behind." Tugging the camisole aside, she glided her fingertips against the soft swell of her belly. "Come on me. Skin to skin."

Shaking his head. "I can't."

Her hooded lids hovered at half-mast. "Yes, you can."

It would be an insane amount of temptation to take his cock out of his pants.

She sat up. Reaching for his waistband, she popped the top snap. "You look miserable. Let me help."

Holding his breath from nerves, he allowed Christy to unfasten his jeans, one torturous steel snap at a time. Once freed, he tugged the denim low on his hips, his cock stood hard and thick.

With a provocative glance, she licked her palm and grasped the shaft. "We'll both feel better in a minute."

Trapped in her warm embrace, he gave into her. She knelt beside him. Her body swayed. The first wet stroke of her hand traveled the length of him, stopping to caress the crown with the pad of her thumb. Her touch drove him wild. The next stroke, she cupped his balls, gently squeezing them against her palm until heat built. With uninhibited enthusiasm, she leaned over to kiss his lips then used her pretty pink tongue to slick her palm again. She moved closer, allowing him to rub the head of his cock against her soft belly. Within a dozen strokes, he felt light-headed. The moment of climax rushed over him. He tensed, grabbed hold of her hand, and came hard, loving every slippery second of friction.

When he finished, he collapsed at her side, laughing. "I will never forget to buy condoms again."

She laughed, too. "Good."

Reaching for a box of tissues, he cleaned them both up.

They smoothed the bedcovers. Christy reached for one of her baggy T-shirts.

With a gentle tap, he stopped her. "Wear this." Picking his flannel shirt off the floor, he handed it to her. "It's warm." He declined to mention he wanted her scent on a personal item he could hold and enjoy after she left.

She slid her arms inside the sleeves and buttoned the front. The plaid shirt hung past her thighs. "Thanks."

He stretched onto his side and patted the mattress. "Come here."

She snuggled into the crook of his arm, spoon style.

He drew the covers over them and wrapped a heavy arm around her. Having a warm body beside him was a comforting extravagance, seldom indulged. Before a fight, Tex made sure a pretty fan would be allowed access to him. Tex also ensured the women remained strangers and received the revolving-door treatment. They were ushered in and out of his hotel suites with equal ease. Fun for a while, ultimately the routine got lonely. Looking back, he now found it hard to believe he'd been so naive to not realize Tex would eventually treat him with the same disregard as those poor women.

Outside, the storm passed. A crescent moon shone through the clouds.

Christy glanced out the window. "Do you think the road will be plowed tomorrow?"

Stroking her hair, he whispered, "Yes."

"I'll have to go home."

He kissed the crown of her head. "I know."

Turning, she looked at him. "You should visit me in Sioux Falls."

"Why?" he teased.

She giggled. "A bunch of good reasons."

Feigning indifference, he muttered, "Like what?"

"You could visit the campus, look around. I know Leonora would love to see you. You could drop in on Hank's Gym. I checked it out last autumn. They were renovating the building and adding on. Pictures of you were hung all over the place. Best of all, you could visit me on campus and make my roommate jealous as hell."

He didn't want to talk and spoil the moment. She felt so good to be near, and he loved everything she'd said. For a moment, a window onto what might be opened. "Maybe."

"Think about it."

If he were a decent man, he'd make it clear she should go home tomorrow with no hope of seeing him again, but it might be too late. He fantasized about the next time he'd see her. Luscious, sweet, responsive Christy. Damn, he got hard again. They were in an impossible situation. He couldn't tell her the truth and couldn't afford not to.

She snuggled close, brushing a bare thigh against his. "We're not going to sleep much tonight, are we?" Rolling over, she wrapped her arms around his neck and pulled him into a kiss. "I think we should start from the beginning and do it all again."

The sight of her wearing his shirt with her glossy hair spilled across his pillow made him wish he could see this every night. A strong urge to talk to Rio, Drew, or even Gee—anyone who could give him some solid advice about falling in love with an outsider and bringing her into the pack was in order.

Rio performed a blood ritual for his mate Sela, but he didn't know the exact details. With pack secrecy crucial, there were few details he could tell Christy without causing a shitload of other unanswered questions to arise. More importantly, he had no right to force anything as extreme as a lifetime commitment, blood-sharing and wolf-shifting on an unsuspecting eighteen-year-old enjoying her first major crush. It wouldn't be fair. Those changes were profound, and after they were made, there would be no going back. He owed it to her to be patient, responsible, and silent on the Wolf matter.

"Mitchell, a few times tonight when I looked into your eyes, I got the sense you're dying to say something."

He reeled. Her intuition was as keen as a Wolf's. Grabbing the first words that popped into his head. "I'm glad you're here."

"That's sweet, but it's not what you were thinking. I'm good at reading people. You were troubled a moment ago. I saw it in your eyes. Is this too weird? Me in your bed all night?"

"It's not that."

"Isn't it? I show up unannounced. Then come on strong. Maybe you have regrets?"

A flood of unsettling emotions swamped him. "No regrets on my part."

"I want you to know I don't need to be babysat. I came here on my own. Tomorrow, I'll leave. Even if tonight is all I get with you, it's worth it." Placing a finger under his chin, she glided his face to hers. "You don't have to think ahead, make promises or plans. I just wanted a bit of you with no strings attached."

"Christy...."

"I have plans, too."

Stunned, he realized he *wanted* strings attached. Christy was the closest he'd ever come to meeting his match, but the Wolf inside felt possessive and sought commitment. He had nothing to offer and no way he could safely share his secret. At the moment, he considered the inner Wolf a huge liability. Yet he couldn't hold back. "Leave a little room in those plans."

Running her fingers through her hair. "What do you mean?"

He grazed his lips against the warm pulse of her throat, longing to make a claim bite. "I'll just keep kissing you until you figure it out."

The kiss deepened. He fought the urge, but before he could stop himself, he bit. Teasing the tender skin with his teeth, he sucked on the warm flesh below her ear. Scorching desire shot through him. Every muscle tensed. God, he wanted her.

"Ouch!" She giggled. "Be careful. You're going to leave your mark on me."

Chapter Five

S he woke to the rumble of an engine on the street below. After prying her sleep-weary eyes open, Christy glanced out the window. An icy-gray sky shone against early morning light. A snowplow blew a white rooster tail of snow into the air. Tapping the mattress beside her, she discovered the bed warm but empty where Mitchell had lain.

"Mitchell?" She reached for the glass of water on the nightstand.

He walked into the room dressed in wet boots, jeans, and a down vest that accentuated the breadth of his shoulders. His cheeks flushed from the cold. Slicking a palm across his hair, he looked at her and smiled. "Good news, I found your car before the snow plow did. I dug it out."

"How did you know it was my car?"

"The tangerine paint job and a red silk daisy in the cup holder tipped me off."

"Ah."

"Guess what I'm thinking?"

"I'm going to hope it involves coffee."

"It can. Do you have to be anywhere this morning?"

"I should go home, do some laundry and say good-bye to my mom. I have to be on campus tomorrow morning."

He crossed the room. "Let's have breakfast and take a short hike."

"All I have is what I wore. I don't have hiking clothes."

His eyes shimmered. "It's not a hike so much as a walk to the edge of town. Your boots will be fine. I'll loan you a coat." Leaning over, he kissed the top of her head. "Get dressed and meet me downstairs."

"Okay." She watched in silence as he left the room. Reaching toward the nightstand, she grabbed her purse. Digging through the deep tote, she located her phone and then clicked it on to call her mom.

Breathless, Mara answered on the second ring. "Christy, are you okay? I've been tracking the storm on the Weather Channel."

"I'm fine. I'm waiting on the snowplow. If you have errands to do today, go ahead. I might be back later than I thought."

"How late?"

"I'm not sure."

A long pause. "The reason I ask is Bob wants to take me to a movie."

For years, her mother denied herself anything like a social life. "Bob the contractor?"

"Yeah, it's not like a date or anything, it's just lunch and a movie."

"Really?" Bob was a good-looking man in his late forties and a former Marine. "It sort of sounds like a date."

"He asked last night, and I said I'd think about it."

"Mom, go and have a good time. It would make me happy to know you're having fun. I'll call you from the road, okay?"

"All right, sweetheart. By the way, where did you spend the night?"

"Ummmm." She stalled. "Above a bar."

"What?"

"Bye, Mom!" Clicking the phone off, she climbed out of bed then gathered her clothes and went into the bathroom to dress. Brushing her hair from her face, she saw Mitchell had left a rosy love-bite on the side of her throat. The mark wasn't pronounced or vicious-looking, but an observant eye would notice. Hunting through her purse, she wished she'd brought some concealer but found mascara and lip gloss instead.

Once she exited Mitchell's room and started down the stairs, it became impossible to avoid a comparison to last night. A post-apocalyptic quiet hung over Gee's Bar. The billiard tables were empty and silent. No music played. In the bar area, the blinds were closed, but a light shone under in the kitchen door. The clatter of pans alerted her others were busy inside. Just as she prepared to call out to them, an indignant growl behind the kitchen door brought her to a halt.

"Those are my blueberries," Gee grumbled. "I picked those and fought off the damn sneaky raccoons. Put them back in the freezer where you found them."

"Come on, Gee." Mitchell's voice floated under the door. "Don't be such a hard ass. I promise I'll replace the berries. I want to make pancakes for Christy. It's a surprise."

"It certainly is!" Gee spoke like he was chewing gravel. "Why does she get to eat my blueberries? Get her out of here! Did my warning not sink in? Boy, you're sitting on a haystack playing with matches."

"I want to do things right. Tell Drew that Christy spent the night in my room."

"Technically, it's my room. Drew won't like it any better."

"I couldn't send her into the storm!"

"It got roaring wild downstairs, do you think she heard or saw anything?"

"No, we were together the whole time."

"You're young. I get it, but, Mitchell, don't go stupid on me."

"Can I have a few blueberries?"

"For pretty Miss Killgaren, how can I say no? But get her gone within the hour."

She froze trying to sift through the confusing content of the conversation. Hearing heavy footsteps, she realized someone shoved the kitchen door. Leaping backward she scurried into the billiard room and hovered in the doorway.

The door swung wide. Gee lumbered into the bar, his silhouette massive. He sniffed the air, his shoulders tensed. Turning, he looked at her and grunted. "We'll have the road plowed to the highway by noon. You'll need to leave before the snow turns to slush."

Mitchell peered through the open door. When he saw her, a bright smile lit his face. "Christy, I made a fresh pot of coffee. Join me in—"

Gee lifted his palms into the air as if a gun were

thrust to his back. "Hold on! My kitchen is a sacred space."

"Don't worry. I won't go into the kitchen." She walked to a booth near a window with the blinds drawn.

"I'll get the coffee." Mitchell returned to the kitchen.

"No. I'll do it." Gee ambled over to the coffeemaker, poured a mug, and brought it to her. "There's cream and sugar on the table." He set the steaming cup in front of her. "You like Mitchell don't you?"

"Yes."

Gee placed a broad hand on the table. "I know he likes you because it's obvious to me that he's never made pancakes before. Try to look pleased when you taste them." He walked into the billiard room.

She sipped the black coffee. A few minutes later, Mitchell returned holding two steaming plates stacked high with pancakes topped with a lava flow of melting butter and syrup. Pride radiated from his face as he set a plate in front of her. "I hope you'll like them."

Picking up a fork, she smiled until her face ached. "I'm sure I will." The pancakes were huge, each the size of the skillet and at least two fingers thick. Puffy and domed they resembled the caps of giant toadstools. Spearing one with the fork tines, she found it springy and resistant to cutting. The first bite confirmed something odd. "Oh, this is different, sort of like a blueberry omelet."

He took a bite and frowned. "I worked without a recipe. Maybe I didn't whisk the eggs long enough?"

"How many eggs did you use?"

"Fourteen."

"Oh. More of a berry soufflé." She took another bite and smiled. "Thank you. I love the blueberries, too."

A big grin lingered on his face.

She ate as much as she could of the filling breakfast, stopping often to sip coffee and talk with Mitchell. His pancake triumph put him in a bubbly mood. Wanting to see him in daylight, she opened the blinds.

"Are you punishing me?" He squinted against the glare of snow and laughed. "You realize if others see us sitting here, they'll want breakfast, too."

Pushing her plate aside, she focused on him. "There's enough left to share. I wanted to see your eyes in daylight."

He leaned across the table and rested on his elbows, looking at her. "You have beautiful eyes."

The way he looked at her teased every tender emotion. "They're plain old hazel."

"Not at all. I see a little blue-green, flecks of gold, and kindness."

She gazed into his eyes, brushing her fingertips against his. He faced east giving her the advantage of looking into their liquid depths. Translucent shades of cinnamon and something resembling pure animal vitality shone bright in his gaze. She'd seen the same look before in the eyes of an impressive male wolf that had been lured inside Reverend Simon's ramshackle compound and trapped. With a shotgun aimed at its head, the wolf stared at his captors with unsettling calm before springing into the air like a rocket and leaping over the compound fence. Shouts and gunfire exploded, but all shots missed. The wolf fled unscathed. Inspired by the defiant act, she began to believe she could escape, too.

He stood and cleared the plates from the table. "Let's take a walk."

"In all this snow?"

"We can drive my four-wheeler part of the way."

"Hurray for that."

Mitchell took the plates into the kitchen. She waited by the front door.

When he returned, he pointed to a red down coat hanging in the foyer. "I brought that downstairs for you."

"What are you going to wear?"

Zipping his vest. "I'll be fine." He took her hand as he pushed the door open. "I'm parked in back. Be careful and don't slip on the steps."

They stepped into blazing sunlight. The snowplow left a hint of diesel in the otherwise-pristine air.

He led her around the side of the building. "The one good thing about a spring storm is a quick thaw." He unlocked the passenger's side of a big blue truck, opened the door, and helped her climb in. The interior had the chill of a refrigerator. She blew warm breath on her hands.

He entered the driver's side. "I'll get the heater going."

"Please do."

"This isn't half-bad. I got up before dawn to dig the cars out when the temps were brutal."

"What time did you wake up?"

"I never actually slept." He tapped a fingertip to his temple. "My mind wouldn't stop working." Leaning close, he kissed her cheek. "You smell good,

Christy." A blinding smile lit his face. "What's your ancestry?"

She laughed. "Wow, that was random! I wish I had a dollar for every time someone said, you smell good. What's your ancestry? I'd have a dollar by now."

"Well?"

"Scottish-Swedish on my mother's side. I never really knew my father. He was Canadian with a little Native American mixed in. You're part Lakota-Sioux, aren't you?"

He put the key in the ignition, turned the engine over, and put the truck in reverse. "Yep."

"Another thing we have in common." She glanced ahead. "Where are we going?"

"A couple miles up this road and over the next hill."

She shivered. "A couple miles? I'm freaking grateful we're not walking the whole way."

"We still have a short hike."

"It's a lazy Sunday. I'm full of pancakes. Don't go Adventure-Man on me. I won't be able to keep up."

The road leading away from Los Lobos had already been plowed. Mitchell's truck rumbled uphill with ease. At a turnoff, they headed up a steep, snowy road into thick woods. A slow bumpy climb ended on a ridge crowned in pines. He turned off the engine and set the brake. "We're here."

The ridgeline looked exactly like the last. "Is this place special to you?"

"You can't see it yet. The cabin is on the south side of the hill."

They walked in thick drifts of snow. He noticed she struggled. Patting his back, he motioned for her to jump aboard. "I'll give you a piggyback ride. It will be faster."

"Okay." She leaped onto his back, grasping his shoulders and wrapping her legs around his hips.

He swayed and staggered a step, laughing.

"Are you sure about this? Yesterday you walked with a limp. This morning you seem fine. Don't overdo it."

"I'm good." He tromped through the snow on sturdy legs. Soon, they crested the ridge. Tucked within a grove of pines she saw a rustic cabin. "That's my family's home. I was born there. A road used to lead straight to the cabin from another ridge, but it washed out and hasn't been repaired in years. The cabin's remained empty." He bent low to set her gently on the ground and dug through his pockets for keys. Approaching the front door, he kicked a drift of snow aside with his boot then unlocked it. When he pushed the door open, chilled musty air enveloped them. "Come in."

She entered and looked around. Though dusty and neglected, the cabin had big potential. High exposed-beam ceilings and lots of south facing windows made it beautiful. Two glaring flaws were also present. Red spray-painted graffiti on a wood-panel walls that read *Fuck Runners* and a hole in the paneling as if someone punched their fist through it.

Tracing her fingers across the angry words. "Vandals? Why are they so mad at runners?"

"Runners were...." He appeared to be searching for words. "Community members who decided for whatever reasons they weren't going to put up with shit anymore and broke from the leadership of the group."

"I'm not sure I understand. Are you a Runner?"

"Yes, as a child. Both my parents lived most of their lives on or near this mountain, and they would have stayed except things got bad. A man named Magnum Tao took charge of the group—"

"Magnum? Really? God, that name sounds like a problem right off the bat."

"Magnum abused power and did all sorts of evil shit."

"Why did people put up with him?"

"They were intimidated. Why did those other men join Reverend Simon?"

"The weak and wicked draw together."

"My parents didn't want my sister and me growing up around this crap. So we moved—*Ran* to Sioux Falls. For several years, we rented the cabin to family or friends, but Magnum couldn't bear it. He scared off every tenant and tore the bridge down that crossed the gully. Cut the power. Took a hatchet to the water heater and the stove, blah, blah, blah."

"I'm not saying he should have, but why not burn the cabin down?"

"That wouldn't have worked for Magnum. He wanted us living under his thumb, especially my poor mother. He was dangerous, but he's dead now. A few months ago, I came back here. Took a look around and promised myself I'd start fixing the place up as soon as spring came." In the kitchen, he pulled out a beautifully crafted drawer. "My dad made these. He did great cabinetwork. That's one reason I want to reclaim this place."

She opened and closed several solid drawers. "Beautiful work."

"I wanted to show you this."

"I'm flattered. I can see it means a lot."

"Christy, I want you to know you're not alone. I had a...." He glanced at his boots. "Not a normal childhood. We kept secrets. Lived on the run. My childhood ended too soon."

Touching her hand to his. "I think that's why we 'get' each other."

"I think you're right." A storm of emotion rolled across his brow. "The next thing I have to say isn't easy. I'm sure I'll hate myself for being an idiot, but I'm going to ask you to go home and forget about me."

Scanning his face for signs of humor gone awry, she saw none. "What? No way!"

"Hear me out. Go back to campus. I want you to have a taste of normal life. Date different guys. Find out what you like."

"I like you."

He rocked on his heels, nervous and unsteady. "I'm scaring myself with how much I already feel for you."

"Good, so there's no problem."

Grasping her hand tight. "There's a big problem. Last night, I lay awake trying to think of a solution that would be fair to you. I've shared a few of my secrets but not all of them. I can't. Not yet."

"You can—"

"Wait. Once you've finished college and seen more of the world, if you want to come back to this cabin, I'll be here."

With hands pressed to his face, she rose on tiptoe. "Mitchell, I'll go home today without a fight. Not because I need to see more of the world or date other guys, but because I'm going to give you the time and space you need to realize we belong together."

"Christy, you don't know," his voice became ragged.

"I know what I want. I'm more adaptable than you think." She pressed a kiss to his lips. "Take as long as you need, and when you're ready, tell me your secret."

Chapter Six

Surrounded by textbooks and paper cups of stale coffee, Christy sat cross-legged on the bed with her laptop snuggled close. She'd reread the same lines again and again. Study time had proved useless all week. Nothing sank in.

Since saying good-bye to Mitchell the previous Sunday, she'd waited for some form of communication, but none came.

Before parting, she'd scribbled her personal information onto a notepad, phone number, e-mail, Instagram account, her address, anything he might be comfortable using to send the smallest message. Folding the note in half, she gave it a kiss for luck and slipped it inside his vest.

Mitchell haunted her every thought. Vivid memories of his soothing voice, what he'd said, and how he said it, tormented her. The weeklong silence between them roared in her ears. She wanted contact, but not in a frantic way. A certain calm hung over the situation. A bone-deep sense of fate convinced her she'd never settle for another. With patience, she would wait for him to come to the same conclusion. Even asking her to leave him had been his idea of an act of love. She knew he'd meant to spare her something, but what?

After closing the laptop, she glanced out the window. She should get away from the empty apartment for a while and take a walk. Her roommate, Alex stayed at her boyfriend's until Sunday night. Saturday afternoons were so lonely.

Knuckles rapped on the door.

Startled, she jumped and ran to look through the peephole. Mitchell's dark eyes gazed back at her. He smiled and waved.

"Hold on!" With trembling hands, she unlatched the three locks her mother put in place for extra security. Mitchell stood on the second-floor balcony, looking shower fresh with damp hair brushed away from his face and a small package wrapped in silver paper clutched in his hands. Taking hold of his wrist, she gave a gentle tug. "Come in."

He entered. "Am I interrupting?"

"No." Shutting the door, she drew the latch and turned to drink in the vision. He looked so handsome in a blue-plaid shirt that complimented the indigo undertones of his black hair. His eyes sparkled. The line of his mouth tensed as if suppressing a smile or laugh. Fumbling with the package in his hands, he appeared nervous.

"You found me."

He nodded. An indecipherable variety of emotions welled beneath the surface, threatening to boil.

"What are you doing in Sioux Falls?"

"Buying a water heater," his voice shook as he

said it.

"It's a long drive for something like that."

Stepping toward her, he thrust the package into her hands. "For you."

With care, she tore the edge of the paper free and saw a book. *Who's Who in Doctor Who; An Ardent Fan's Guide To All Things Whovian.* He looked embarrassed. "I'm sorry. I don't know why I bought it."

She smiled until her cheeks ached. "I'll read it. Thank you, Mitchell."

He dipped his chin and drew a deep breath. "Christy, I want you to know I fall asleep thinking of you and you're the first thing I think about when I open my eyes."

"Really?"

His gaze locked to hers. The innocence in his eyes melted, instantly replaced with fierce passion. "I know it's selfish and wrong, but I don't think I'm going to be able to stay away from you."

Stunned, she stared at the soft shadows on his face.

He stepped closer. "I'll be your friend, protector, lover or whatever you wish. I'll even wait for you if that's what you want. I needed to say this face-to-face."

Stroking her fingertips across his temple, she couldn't hold back. She leaped into his arms. Wrapping her legs around his waist, she gave him a bear hug and squealed with joy.

Laughing, he turned in a slow circle. "I'm so happy to see you."

She planted a flurry of kisses against mouth, jawline, and throat. The buttons on his shirt were plucked free and a patch of silky hair fondled. "Take me to bed."

"What?" he sounded breathless.

"You're not the only one who falls asleep with someone on their mind. I want to spend the rest of the weekend with you behind locked doors."

He froze. "Christy, are you sure? I didn't come here to pressure you."

She skimmed her hands across his chest. "Mitchell, I'm absolutely sure."

"I won't argue." He motioned toward the two bedroom doors. "Which room is yours?"

Both doors were open. "Take a guess."

"I see a lot of orange in the room on the right."

"It's not orange; it's saffron. That's my Bollywood decor. Good guess."

Carrying her into the bedroom, he kicked the door shut. "Where's your roommate?"

"Gone until Sunday."

"Lucky us." He dropped her lightly onto the mattress then finished unbuttoning his shirt and shed it. In a flash, he stripped his boots and belt away, kicking everything aside.

Reaching for the top snap on his jeans, she unfastened it. "I thought I'd have to have to come to you."

"Here I am."

"Open the nightstand drawer."

Leaning over, he pulled the drawer open. "How many lip balms can one person use?"

"That's only half my collection. The rest are in the bathroom."

"Ah-ha." He picked up a box of condoms that came in bright colors and read it aloud, "Tropical

Temptations. Wild guess, we use the orange one first?"

She tugged the hoodie over her head, revealing lots of skin and a lacy pink bra. "It's saffron, and yes."

He set the box on the nightstand, drew the bed covers aside, and motioned for her to climb beneath.

Not feeling particularly graceful, she rolled under the covers and wriggled her yoga pants down her legs, tossing them aside. He slid into bed beside her with his feet hanging over the end.

With a gentle touch, he cupped her face in his hands and gazed at her. "I know in the past you were.... Not treated—"

"Abused. It's okay to say it."

"I care about you. You'd tell me, wouldn't you, if you wanted me to stop?"

"For years, I felt broken. I worried I might panic or feel shame when someone touched me. In your bed, I felt safe, loved...and fixed. Mitchell, I know I'm ready, and it has to be you."

He wrapped his arms around her and drew her against his chest. "I drove myself crazy all week, thinking about you dating other guys, or God forbid, one of them taking my place next to you in—"

"Hush." She held a finger to his lips.

Pulling her beneath him, he rested his weight on his elbows and leaned close to kiss her lips. A look of pure love softened his face. "Christy, my heart's wide open."

Breathless, she wrapped her legs around his, reveling in the sensation of Mitchell's warm body pressed against hers. Returning his kiss with lips parted, she tangled her fingers in his hair and held him. The kiss deepened. A hint of wintergreen traveled on his breath.

He slid a bra strap from her shoulder and pushed the fabric lower, exposing a breast. In slow succession, his kisses traveled down the side her cheek to the tender hollow at the base of her throat until he buried his face between her breasts. With a mouth soft as silk, he explored every inch of bare skin with kisses. When his lips came to rest on her nipple, he circled it with the tip of his tongue, leaving it glossy. She closed her eyes in bliss as he gave the nipple a gentle tug past his lips and sucked. The burst of pleasure left her arching beneath him. His actions were unrushed. Making contented sounds, he brought the nipple to a fiery peak before switching to its twin.

His kisses swept lower, tickling her belly with his warm breath. Her anticipation built as he took hold of her hips and pulled her near. Dipping his face between her thighs, he brushed his nose against her springy curls. "I love your scent."

She clenched the pillow and dug her fingers into it. Ready to writhe and go wild, she willed herself to relax into the stunning sensations of Mitchell making love to her. His wet kisses and languid tongue strokes left her breathless. She wanted him to linger on the crazy little spot above her clit. As her excitement soared, she caressed his denim-clad leg with her bare foot. "Time to ditch the pants," she pleaded.

Lifting his weight off her, he unsnapped the fly and tugged the jeans down his legs. Undressing beneath the covers proved difficult, and soon, he tangled in the bedding, laughing. She assisted by kicking the pants to the floor.

Mitchell reached toward the nightstand and

unwrapped the box of condoms. He removed the orange packet. "Lucky tangerine." He kissed the foil before ripping it open with his teeth. His erection curved toward his belly. He capped the condom over the head with his fist, rolling the vibrant-colored condom down the shaft with quick, short strokes.

Her gaze riveted on his actions and the slender trail of hair that ran from his chest to his abs and ended at the thick patch of dark hair.

He noticed where her gaze focused and patted a reassuring hand against her thigh. "I'll go slow. If you need to, tell me to stop." Kneeling between her thighs, he eased her onto her back with a gentle tap. He grabbed a pillow and tucked it under her hips. "I'm going to stay where I can watch you, okay?" Leaning onto his elbows, he kissed her mouth. The faint tang of her own flavor hovered on his lips. Taking hold of her hand, he guided it to his shaft. "When you're ready, put me inside you. We'll move together."

Closing her eyes, she rubbed him against her. An intense thrill shot straight to her core. With a slight adjustment to the angle, he slid inside with ease. The initial stretch paired with wet friction delivered exquisite sensations.

Clasping his hands with hers, he sank deeper and paused. "Are you okay?"

"Oh, yes."

Their fingers locked. He withdrew in increments and pressed again with a slow, teasing pace, each stroke smooth and slick. For many minutes, they moved together at the same sweet, slow pace that honey poured. She loved the intimate privilege of witnessing Mitchell's rugged face enthralled by bliss.

During an unguarded moment, his dark lashes fluttered.

Gently breaking his grip, she smoothed her hands across the rippling muscles of his back. "I'm right there," she whispered, needing the slightest push.

He wrapped his arms around her, as if gripping a life raft. Every muscle tensed. A burst of energy uncoiled within, making his hips race. Rising on trembling arms, he arched his throat and came with a broken cry. Moments passed before he eased his weight against her.

She drew him close and caressed the swooping curves of his buttocks. He buried his face in her hair and allowed himself to be held as he gulped breath in panting bursts. For a moment, she wondered if his ragged gasps might be a sob. Sensing he needed reassurance, she kissed his cheek. "It's good."

"Christy." His voice dropped to a quiet rumble. "I want to be someone you can be proud of. I'm not sure how, but I'm going to make things work."

"Mitchell, I've seen you at your best. I am proud of you."

A sunny smile curled the corners of his mouth. They lay together, lacking the will to move until he slid free of her. He removed the condom, wrapped it in tissue, and tossed it into the wastebasket.

Rolling onto her side, she propped her weight on her elbow. "I have a great idea. Why don't we get dressed, go to the pizza parlor across from the campus, get a monster-sized pizza, and bring it back here? It's quicker to pick it up, and only a couple blocks away."

***

The chilly afternoon shadows were long. Walking at Mitchell's side, she looked up often to catch a glimpse of his profile. The pizza parlor was packed when they arrived. "Jeez, I forgot it's Saturday."

"It's okay." He pushed the door open, and they walked inside. A mob of diners filled the foyer along with the enticing aromas of good food.

Several familiar faces were spotted on entry. She recognized a girl from a journalism class. "Hi, Trish!"

Trish elbowed her way over. "Did you get your projects finished during spring break?"

She shook her head. "Not yet."

With her mouth agape, Trish stared at Mitchell. "I know you." A young man rushed to her side. "This is my boyfriend, Scott."

Scott appeared awed. "Wail'n Waya!" He dug through his jacket pocket and pulled out his phone. "Dude, can I get a picture with you?" Slamming himself against Mitchell's arm, he leaned close and took several photos. "Thanks. I always thought you were great. I'm really sorry you've had such a shitty year." He muttered, "I'm posting these to Facebook ASAP." He scanned Mitchell. "You look good. Maybe it's time to start fighting again? I spent a fucking fortune on pay-per-view because of you. I can't believe you just walked in here. This is epic. Wail'n Waya everybody!" Pointing at Mitchell, he shouted, "The cage king!"

Waving his hand, Mitchell winced. "Please don't...."

People craned their necks to look. A few rose from their seats to get a better view.

Mitchell appeared terribly uncomfortable. "Maybe we should go?"

"It's okay. Be cool. I'll order the pizza." She slipped away.

Within moments, a crowd gathered around Mitchell, waiting for their chance to take a picture with him or ask for an autograph.

Christy ordered an XXL four-cheese pepperoni with black olives pizza while Mitchell handled the rush of attention like a pro. He indulged all photo requests and even managed to appear dignified while some teenager boys shot video.

The moment the finished pizza slid across the steel countertop, she paid, grabbed the box, and headed toward the front door. "Come on, Mitchell, let's go."

He looked weary. "Thank God."

***

Sitting beside Mitchell on the couch, she finished her second piece of pizza. They were well into the evening's second episode of *Doctor Who* when the phone rang. Her mother's number displayed. She clicked.

"Hi, Mom, what's up?"

"Christy." Mara's tone was terse. "Are you watching TV?"

"Yeah."

"I'm worried."

"About what, Mom?"

"About the horrid breaking news exclusive TM3 exposé I'm watching!"

"Mom, I don't watch scandal news shows. It's

exploitation. Celebrity DUI mug shots. Kardashians having wardrobe malfunctions in airports. Who cares?"

"You should care. Tonight's breaking news is about you and that young man."

"Hold on, Mom." She turned. "Mitchell put on TM3. Something is going on."

Mitchell looked disappointed. "I would never watch that crap." He changed the channel.

The TM3 set was designed to look like an editorial bullpen of a legitimate news agency except the "journalists" all had pumpkin-colored spray tans and hipster clothing. The two women were cute but whiny.

The man's big-capped teeth made him look like crocodile doing its best Walter Cronkite impersonation. "TM3 exclusive! Tonight, we dig deeper into a lurid case that captured the nation's attention and put fear in every parent's heart. After nearly four years of court-ordered silence, we now know the face and name of that poor girl involved in the infamous Reverend Simon kidnapping...."

A photo flashed on the screen of Christy, carrying the pizza.

"Oh no!" She groaned.

"Christine Killgaren is now a healthy, happy eighteen-year-old college freshman, living off campus, but she can't seem to stay out of trouble. TM3 has this exclusive footage of her cuddling at a campus pizza parlor with another of South Dakota's infamous characters, Wail'n Waya, the controversial ex-cage fighter and scandal magnet. These two sure look like an item."

A bubble-headed blonde in a tight pink T-shirt

interrupted. "Rumor has it Wail'n Waya testified in court against Reverend Simon and his henchmen, and that he is, in fact, the man who saved Christine Killgaren from an execution-style slaying in a dark business park." She made duck lips at the camera. "I think it's pretty heroic."

She stared in horror at the screen. "Somebody videoed us walking back to the apartment. They showed the building's address!"

"Christy!" Mara shouted. "Are you still there? I want you out of the apartment ASAP."

"Try to stay calm, Mom. I'm going to go." She clicked the phone off. It immediately rang again. It was her roommate. She allowed the call to go to voice mail.

"Christy, it's Alex. I'm seeing some weird shit on Facebook about you and some martial arts guy. I know how freaked you get about privacy. Our apartment number is posted. Just check it out."

The phone rang again. Leonora's number displayed. She clicked. "Hi."

"Christy, I have to bring a serious safety concern to your attention."

"I know. I'm watching TV."

"Honey, this goes beyond the footage on TM3. A twitter thread has popped up of mostly your classmates offering their support, which is great, but several are giving away your schedule and location on a typical day. It's done in innocence, but they do mention teachers, classes, and places you meet. Be careful."

Her hands shook. "I will."

"Is Mitchell with you?"

"Yes."

"Good. Change your routine. Don't go to class next week. I'm going to call Mara. We'll make other plans, okay?"

"Okay." She clicked the phone off and looked at Mitchell. "Leonora sounds worried. I wonder if she's not telling me everything. After Reverend Simon's conviction, the FBI received dozens of letters from crackpots blaming me and promising revenge. I'm not sure the letters ever stopped."

***

A long fitful night gave way to a clear Sunday morning.

She woke with Mitchell's arms locked around her.

He drew her close to his chest with an expression somber as the morning chill. "I'm not leaving you alone. I want you to come with me." He smoothed the hair from her face and kissed her forehead. "Christy, I'm going to pick up some breakfast for us. While I'm gone, I want you to pack everything you'll need for a few weeks and be ready to go."

"Go where?"

"We'll figure it out. All I know is the safest place for you is with me."

She took hold of his wrist. "Then I'm going with you to get breakfast."

He looked nervous. "There's something important I want to talk to you about."

"What?"

Mitchell reached for his boxers on the floor and stepped into them. "I planned to wait, but the situation forced me to reconsider."

She hunted under the bed and pulled out a duffel bag. "The look on your face is alarming me. Could you give me a hint?"

His expression melted. "I'm different in a special way. I suspect you're a little different, too. Once I say what those differences are, everything changes."

"Mitchell, I think we're alike."

Stepping close, he cupped the sides of her face. "You're right. Looking back it's probably how we found each other. I'm waiting to get permission—"

"Permission for what?"

His mouth tensed. "I need to think about how I'm going to say this. Let's get coffee first."

They finished dressing. He reached for his keys.

"Don't bother. There's a breakfast-burrito food truck that parks on the campus lot. It's literally across the street. I walk there every morning."

He grabbed his coat. "Let's make it fast in case we're recognized again."

After locking the apartment, she wound a sunny peach scarf around her throat. "Mitchell, I'm sorry we got spotted in public and things got crazy, but I'm glad it means I'll be with you."

"Me, too." He smiled.

She led as they descended the staircase. "Hurry up. I'm hungry."

They crossed the street and strode across the parking lot. The trees lining the campus palisade displayed the first signs of spring.

He held her hand. "You walk fast for a girl."

"This is my medium pace." Giggling, she broke from him and bolted toward the food truck. "This is fast!" Glancing over her shoulder, she grinned and then took off at a sprint.

Strolling at a leisurely pace, he enjoyed the sight of her hair streaming behind her as she ran.

A man with a robust build stepped from behind a tree, blocking Christy's path. The sun glinted off the lens of the guy's mirrored sunglasses. His weathered face was expressionless and appeared to be a hardened mask. Dressed head to toe in camouflage, he grasped a slender blade in his fist. With the speed of a striking snake, he grabbed hold of Christy's scarf, knocking her off balance. Arms flailing, she wheeled forward out of control.

In a slow-motion moment of horror, Mitchell watched as the man yanked Christy against him.

"This is for Reverend Simon!" He snarled as he plunged the blade into her abdomen.

Christy smacked hard against the man's fist and shuddered. Her lips parted, but no sound escaped. With a look of shock on her face, she clutched the assailant's hunting vest and clawed the fabric. When he pulled away, her hands flew to her belly as she collapsed onto the pavement.

The attacker darted away, leaving her slumped on the ground with a pool of blood spreading.

"Christy!" Racing toward her, he knelt and scooped her into his arms. Limp as a ragdoll, she didn't have the strength to turn her head.

The man leaped in a dark SUV and, with squealing tires, drove off.

Feeling helpless, he wanted to chase the man and break his neck.

"Mitchell," she mumbled. "I loved you."

Alarmed to hear "loved" past tense, he placed his

palm on the wound to stanch the flow. The gouge in her side left her clothes blood-soaked. The color drained from her lips. Grabbing his cell with slippery fingers, he punched 911. It felt like an eternity before dispatch came on the line.

"We need help!" he shouted. "A woman's been attacked on the Sioux Falls University campus."

"Can you describe the nature of the attack?"

"She's been stabbed in the abdomen. The wound's deep. This is bad. Send help!"

"Remain calm. Where are you?"

"We're near the campus parking lot."

"Which lot?"

Christy groaned and fell silent. Her palm opened to reveal pieces of ripped fabric and thread.

He panicked. "I don't know! Wait, the sign says 'Section I.' I don't know if that's a goddamned one or a capital *I* or a lowercase *L*. We're on a walkway next to some cottonwoods. She's bleeding out fast. You've got to send an ambulance to the campus. Figure out our location on the way. For fuck's sake do something!"

"Don't yell, sir."

He stroked Christy's face with bloodstained fingers. She didn't respond. "She's dying! Get someone here now!"

"Stay on the line. Can you give me a description of your surroundings? What buildings are you close to? Did you witness the assault? Keep talking to me...."

Glancing up, he focused on a blue, cloudless sky, so brilliant a hue it looked like heaven. His gaze returned to Christy. She didn't move, not even the flutter of an eyelash. Placing his fingertips to her throat, he felt for a pulse. Nothing.

A broken sob escaped him. "No!"

He felt her slipping away. The time to bargain or explain passed. Christy's only chance hinged on sharing his secret—and offering the gift.

Digging into his pocket, he retrieved his father's knife, pulled the blade open, and made a slash in his wrist. The wound trickled crimson. The cut stung as he racked his memory for the exact wording to the blessing of the Great Spirit Waya. It had been years since he'd heard his mother recite it.

Part legend, part truth untold generations ago, *Waya* the mysterious spirit of the wolf offered his ancestors the gift of being one with the wolves. He'd heard those born with some wolf blood could be made whole. Rio performed such a ritual for Sela, and it worked. He owed it to Christy to try.

Holding his dripping wrist above her wound, he allowed their blood to mingle. "Christy, come back to me."

A siren howled in the distance, racing closer.

No words to the special blessing came to mind beyond the remembrance the blessing must be offered with sincerity and humility. "I want to put the past behind us and build a future with you," he muttered. "We're supposed to be together." He kissed her lips. They felt cool. "Accept the gift of my blood, and may Waya accept you into the pack."

The kiss deepened into shared breath. He forced warm air into lungs. *Keep her alive.* A silent mantra ran through his head. *Breathe for her.*

The ambulance arrived in a blur of noise, the crash of a gurney, and flashing lights. Two police cars were close behind. In a heartbeat, a crew of professionals surrounded Christy and urged him to move aside. When a bit of fabric fell from her limp hand, he snatched it off the ground and thrust it deep into his pocket.

A paramedic with kind eyes drew him away. "Let us help her."

He released his grip just as Christy opened her eyes.

"Mitchell." She reached for his hand. "I feel so strange." Glancing past him. "The sky is so, so blue."

"Step back." A paramedic clamped an oxygen mask over Christy's face. "We have to stabilize her." They went to work.

Rising on trembling legs, he watched the entire procedure unfold as if he were dreaming. The color returned to Christy's face. She gestured with her hands and lifted the oxygen mask to speak. The paramedic reminded her to remain still and set the mask in place.

A police officer approached. "Are you the man who called this in?"

He felt too distracted by the miracle in front of him to stop and speak with this man, but had no choice "Yes."

The officer pulled a pad and pen from his belt. "Did you witness the assault?"

Christy lifted the oxygen mask. "Brother Jacob, one of Reverend Simon's disciples did this to me! The bastard's covered in my blood." She pointed across the lot. "He drove a blue SUV. He's wearing a camouflage vest."

Plucking a radio off his belt, the officer immediately called the description in.

He stared in awe. She'd been in the arms of

death but wriggled free. Christy sounded so strong he dared to hope Waya accepted her. The next logical question was, would she accept her new life and forgive him for not offering her a choice?

Chapter Seven

Mitchell slumped in the reclining chair beside Christy's hospital bed. Out of kindness, one of the nurses switched the uncomfortable chair with metal armrests for the cozy bed-like chair he'd been dozing in.

With bleary eyes, he watched local newscasts like a zombie. During the last two days, Christy slept beneath a haze of heavy-duty sedatives. Thankfully, she'd be okay. The surgeons remained puzzled by the extent of the damage they'd seen in the ER and offered no explanation for the supernatural speed of healing that occurred.

He didn't plan to enlighten them.

Continuous breaking-news announcements kept waking him. The statewide manhunt underway for the fugitive known as Brother Jacob, the last of Reverend Simon's accomplices to evade justice, remained the top story.

Of course, the breaking news always turned out to be a rehash of old news, but each time he reacted to the flashing red graphic rippling across the screen with a pounding heart. Brother Jacob needed to be caught and punished. Until then, there'd be no peace. It frustrated the hell out of him it wasn't happening fast enough. After a promising start, the trail went cold. Brother Jacob, a seasoned survival expert, had disappeared into a national park. So far, dogs, helicopters, and thermal imaging equipment had turned up nothing.

Promising to stand guard, he'd finally convinced Mara to return to her hotel room to rest in a real bed. The machines at the bedside hummed intermittent beeps, keeping him company.

For the first time in forty-eight hours, Christy opened her eyes and scanned the room. "Mitchell?"

He bolted upright. "I'm here."

She looked confused. "Is my mother here, also? Earlier, I thought I heard her voice."

He rushed to her side and grasped her hand. "I sent her to the hotel to take a nap. She's exhausted."

With soft eyes, she gazed at him. "Who else is here? Is it just us?"

Kissing her fingertips, he gave her hand a gentle squeeze. "Just us. Every hour, a nurse checks in and injects something into your IV bag."

Christy rolled her eyes. "Whatever she's injecting is doing a number on my imagination."

Relief to hear her smoky voice rushed through him. "Are the drugs good?"

"Amazing! Mitchell, I have to tell you something. I know I'll sound crazy. What's happening to me may not be real, but it feels real."

A tingle of alarm shot up his spine. "What?"

"I've been dreaming that I'm becoming a wolf."

He leaned closer. "A wolf?"

"Yes, a real flesh-and-blood wolf! My heart beats

faster. I'm covered in silvery fur. When I'm a wolf I can smell, which nurse is walking into my room. I have the wildest adventures. They're so beautiful. I'm a wolf running through the woods with you. In the dreams, you're a wolf, too."

Fear and hope battled inside. "Wow, I want one of those IV cocktails, too."

"In the dream. We're happy together. We have this whole other life as wolves. It's better than any make-believe game I could have created as a kid."

Tears welled in his eyes. "Just get better, Christy."

"I suppose I sound crazy."

The red graphic for *Breaking News!* flashed across the television screen. He froze.

The strident voice of a male newscaster boomed. "State troopers have discovered what they believe to be the abandoned SUV belonging to felon at large, Brother Jacob...."

An old mug shot of the harsh-faced child kidnapper, sexual predator, and a heap of other offenses blanketed the screen.

"This morning, state police located the blood-stained SUV at the mouth of an inaccessible canyon. Jacob is believed to be traveling on foot and possibly headed for one of the many buried caches of supplies he's said to have been living off for the past four years."

"Holy crap!" Christy wailed. "Is he still on the loose?" She yanked at her IV. "I'm leaving."

He grabbed her hand. "Sweetheart, don't do that."

"He's out there! I know how to find him and the types of places they'd choose for a cache. Reverend

Simon was always ordering someone to dig a bunker somewhere and stock it. It will be deep, too, at least ten feet."

Patting her shoulder. "You're heavily medicated with stitches. You can't go anywhere."

"I can talk to the police. I'm ready. Call a detective. Have him bring maps. Call a nurse. Get this damn IV out of my arm! I don't need it. I want to help."

"So do I." His eyes narrowed on the screen drinking in every detail about the SUVs location. "I'm going to call the officer in charge, and then I have leave for a little while."

"Where are you going?"

"On an errand."

"Would you bring me back a burrito?"

"Sure." He bolted toward the door. "I might be gone for a while."

***

Mitchell released a blast of air from his tires before heading down a rutted fire road on the edge of the national forest. Following the police band conversations had been simple. Getting around the FBI barricades set around the perimeters of the park proved trickier. He'd cut through a wire fence and slipped past on private property.

Bouncing along a dirt road, he sniffed the scent of pine needles on the breeze. The fresh fragrance cleared his head of city smells. The hunt began in earnest. In his mind, Brother Jacob was prey with a bright orange target painted on his forehead.

In the distance, he saw the first signs of activity.

A helicopter circled a wooded canyon then a second helicopter joined the chase. There were no roads leading into this remote area. Using the foot trails or an airlift were the only ways in or out. Having reached the end of the line, he pulled the truck within a grove of trees and parked.

Realizing the authorities were closing in, he hurried to ready himself. As dusk neared, he thought it likely the helicopters and ground search would soon retreat.

Darkness wouldn't stop him. In fact, it was an ally. Locking his wallet and Glock in the glove compartment, he undressed. Taking a long drink from a plastic water bottle, he intended to travel light, no food, water, weapons, but most of all no trace of human Mitchell would be left behind.

If someone spotted his truck, he'd claim to be a concerned loved one, watching the FBI pursuit from a distance.

If he showed up on aerial thermal imagery, no one would blink at the presence of a wolf moving through the woods, not with more pressing matters to deal with like a violent pedophile on the run.

One last thing remained to be done. He removed the tiny shred of hunting vest Christy had managed to rip away with her fingernails, from the cellophane bag he'd placed it in. Holding the reeking bits of thread to his nose, he inhaled. To his heightened senses the scrap of cloth smelled of stale sweat, adrenaline, beer, and a trace of Christy's blood. Beneath it all, Brother Jacob's distinct scent burned deep into his brain.

The Wolf in him wanted justice.

Stepping out of the truck, he hid a key beneath

the front bumper. Calling on the Great Spirit Waya, he silently asked to be granted keener senses and greater strength that he might serve the highest good.

Mumbling the words, "For Christy," he knelt on the ground and shifted to wolf form. With a whimper and crackle of bone, he accomplished the feat in a seamless *swoosh*. Ready for duty, the Wolf appeared. With an amber sun sinking fast, he trotted beneath the cover of trees sniffing the ground for signs of Jacob.

A single helicopter continued to circle the south-facing wall of the canyon, so he headed in that direction. Soon it grew dark, and the helicopter returned to its home base. Without the choppy *whomp, whomp, whomp* of the helicopter's spinning blades to create aural clutter, he tuned into the sounds of the wind, the dry rustle of rabbits darting through brush, the occasional screech of an owl, but no human sounds greeted his sensitive wolf ears.

Following a seldom-used trail overgrown by bramble, he descended into a canyon. Deer prints were the most common feature on the track. Then he saw a big boot print with a tiny avalanche of silt above. Glancing uphill, he spotted the place where a man slid down a steep grade landing in the middle of the path.

Excitement rose. The prints were fresh and the scent ripe. He'd picked up Brother Jacob's trail. From here, the pursuit came with ease. Recent rain left the ground impressionable to footprints. Moisture held the scent. He raced forward, holding his intentions in mind. Jacob deliberately harmed Christy and even took pleasure in his brutality. He'd have no qualms about nixing the bastard.

A copse of trees near the base of the canyon caught his attention. Leaving the trail, he headed toward the grove. Immediately, his senses were assaulted by the odor of urine, the tang of sweat in the air, and, most telling, the gamy aroma of canned meat stew.

Without doubt, Brother Jacob was near, but where? The area beneath the trees appeared barren except for leaf litter. Sniffing the ground, his paws brushed the edges of a trapdoor. Below, he heard the hollow rattle of a spoon scraping inside a can.

Elated he'd found a cache with its grubby prize still inside, he considered how best to get in. Then he realized he didn't have to. Jacob would come to him.

Throwing his head back, he wailed a booming wolf call that echoed through the canyon. He stood back and waited. Nothing happened. He howled again. This time the noises inside the bunker stopped.

A faint, "Goddamn it," could be heard along with the *clink* of a can being tossed.

Pawing at the hidden door, he exposed a camouflaged net covered in leaves and shredded it. Once he denuded the door of cover, he scratched his claws against the wood, barking and making loud snuffling sounds. He bayed again for good measure, ending in a string of annoying *yip, yip, yip, yips*. Leaping into the air, he landed hard on top of the door, which made a rumbling *thud* when his weight connected. The wood flexed. He jumped again, landing as forcefully as his agile wolf body would allow. Catching his breath, he leaped back and thundered a booming howl.

The trapdoor burst open accompanied by a

scattered cloud of leaf debris and a slew of sour odors. "Get the fuck out of here, buzzard bait!" Brother Jacob popped his head above ground with a gun pointed toward the trail.

Hidden behind the raised door, it took every bit of willpower to not lash out at the back of Jacob's head. Instead, he waited with muscles coiled, prepared to spring.

"Goddamn pest, where are you?" Hoisting himself out of the hole, Jacob scanned the hillside. The foul residues of alcohol and fear shellacked his skin.

Crouched an arm's length away, he released an involuntary growl of disgust.

Jacob turned. His jaw dropped.

Explosive as cannon fire, he sprang full force, arching through the air and slammed into Jacob.

With his arms wind milling, Jacob staggered and dropped the gun.

Riding the leap's momentum, Mitchell knocked the target of his fury onto his back, landing heavy on the man's chest. He clamped his fanged jaws around the bastard's throat. With the satisfying snap of a steel trap, his teeth sank deep and tore skin and sinew. Jacob thrashed, grabbing handfuls of fur to no effect, his screams turned to horrid, wet gurgles.

The wolf in him raged as blood fountained from the jugular. Biting and growling, he shredded flesh. Too soon, all movement stopped. The kidnapper, child-rapist, and would-be assassin lay still on the ground, mouth agape with glassy eyes staring skyward at nothing.

Justice accomplished.

Drenched in blood, he limped to the bottom of

the canyon where he'd caught the scent of fresh water. Killing Christy's tormentor left him an uneasy victor. He wanted to be rid of all trace of Jacob on his fur. With a whimper, he hobbled down the steep canyon where he found a rushing stream.

Stepping into the icy water sobered him. He'd just killed a man. A man who deserved to die. *What will Christy think of the Wolf in me?* He worried she'd be frightened or repelled once she knew what he was capable of.

Lowering his head to the bubbling stream, he lapped a long drink, rinsing the thick taste of blood from his muzzle. Rolling in the current, he bathed his coat, hoping someday his soul might wash clean of all stain as well. It would be both a relief and disturbing to tell Christy she no longer had to worry about Brother Jacob. The deed spared her another round of endless court dates. He just wished he'd not taken so much pleasure in killing the bastard.

Once the blood washed free, he shook the water from his coat and started the long trot back to his truck. If he hurried, he could shower and get a couple hours of sleep at the hotel.

***

Mitchell woke midmorning. Once he'd fallen asleep in a real bed, he went down hard into a dreamless oblivion. Eager to check in, he dressed in clean clothes. He crept into Christy's hospital room, holding a brown paper bag of warm, foil-wrapped burritos.

Christy was watching television.

"Mitchell." She smiled the moment she saw him,

and his heart filled. Pointing at the screen, she appeared agitated. "You won't believe what happened."

He glanced at the TV. The news played looped footage of state troopers and rescue crews descending on the canyon. A helicopter airlifted a body wrapped in a yellow blanket out of the ravine.

"The authorities are pretty sure they found Brother Jacob's body this morning in a wilderness area."

"Pretty sure?" His gaze narrowed on the screen. "That looks like a body in a bag to me."

"His face is so badly maimed, forensics will need to confirm Jacob's identity." She paused to brush her fingertips across his brow. "Mitchell, you look exhausted."

He handed her the sack. "I brought you a couple breakfast burritos with scrambled eggs."

She grabbed one. "Thanks. I'm starving. Why don't you take the other?"

He took the second burrito and unwrapped it. "Has anyone mentioned how Brother Jacob died?"

"Possible bear mauling. They found his throat torn open. Definitely an animal."

Swallowing a bite of food before he choked. "Wolf."

"Are there wolves in that area?"

"No."

She looked puzzled. "Then it's likely a bear."

"Wolf."

Christy blanched. "You sound certain."

He dreaded her next reaction might be disgust. "I am."

"Is this connected to your secret?" She drew a

shaky breath. "The one you couldn't share?"

"Yes."

"Does this have something to do with your eyes flashing amber when you're angry?"

"It does."

With a creased brow, she looked concerned as she set the burrito down. "Did the avenging angel do this?"

"Yes." He tensed. "With no regrets. I hope you can forgive me."

"Wait!" She glanced around. "Are we alone? Slow down, Mitchell. Are you telling me you killed Brother Jacob and made it look like an animal attack?"

He gazed at the floor. How could he explain?

"It's all right," she whispered. "Brother Jacob was a bad man. He hurt me and many other girls. You did the right thing. I love you for it."

"Christy, I didn't just make it look like a wolf attack. I killed Brother Jacob while in wolf form."

"What?"

"I snuck up to his hiding place and attacked, as a wolf."

"A real wolf? Fangs and paws?"

"Yes. A wolf is a big part of what I am. My ancestors claimed to share blood with the wolves. After you were stabbed and lay dying, to save your life, I shared my blood with you. The blood of Waya is why you're healing so fast."

"You shared blood with me? How?"

"I cut my wrist and mingled my blood with yours. You barely had a pulse. I was scared to lose you. Forgive me for doing such a thing without your consent."

"Mitchell, are you saying you're a wolf, or can

become a wolf? As in the spirit of the wolf?"

"No. I can transform at will and take on the physical shape of a wolf. I become furry and fangy...everything."

She gulped breath. "I don't think I can quite believe any of this."

He smoothed the hair from her face. Her eyes were especially bright and full of life. "You don't need to believe in something for it to be true. Long ago, a sacred pact was made between man and wolf. I sensed the blood of Waya in your veins. Diluted but unmistakable. At least one of your ancestors was a wolf, or else the transformation would not have been possible. I brought you into our ranks, and I'll never abandon you. When you're ready, I want you as my mate. You'll be cherished over a very long lifetime. Christy, you'll change over the next months and become what I am. I hope you can embrace that fact."

She sat in silence for a few moments, looking excited and stunned. "I don't know what to say."

"You don't have to say anything now. Let the idea soak in. There are a lot of advantages. I can prove all of this to you once you're out of the hospital."

"How would you do that?"

"I've already spoken about this to our pack Alpha, Drew. You'll need to be introduced to the pack and asked to swear a vow of secrecy. We'll go into a wilderness area together, and I'll help you through your first wolf-shift."

A quivering smile lit her face. "Sounds romantic."

"I won't kid you. The first few shifts can be painful. You might get scared, but I'll be at your side, offering support and my heart."

"Mitchell, your face is so serious. You're telling the truth, aren't you?"

He nodded.

"I'll keep an open mind." She took hold of his hand, weaving her fingers between his. "It sounds like something special to look forward to."

Kissing her forehead. "It will be."

Epilogue

The Black Hills, Four Months Later

The road leading to Gray Paw Mountain wound higher. The sun slipped behind a ridge casting the Black Hills into purple twilight. For an early July evening, the temperature felt reasonably cool.

Christy sat beside Mitchell in the truck. She held his hand in between his shifting gears. "How much farther?"

"Next ridge." He glanced sideways at her as he drove. "Are you okay? I can take you back to town, and we can do this another time."

She shook her head. "I'm nervous, but I've been ready for weeks."

He laughed. "And I said 'no' because I wanted to make sure you were fully healed."

The past months had presented many challenging but amazing experiences. An unusually short stay in the hospital baffled her doctors. She and Mitchell suspected the blood of Waya had taken root.

Completing her first shift would confirm those suspicions.

Warmth shone in Mitchell's eyes. "Did you wolf-dream last night?"

As soon as she woke in the hospital, lucid dreams of running free on all fours in wolf form became nightly events. "Oh, yes."

A broad smile lit his face. "I dreamed about you."

Squeezing his hand. "I thought about what you said, and the answer is yes. I can stay in Los Lobos until the end of the month. I want to help you work on the cabin. There's no reason to go home sooner. The new semester won't even start until August."

Mitchell stared ahead. "There's something I want to run past you." He paused. "I enrolled in college, too. It's time to get my shit together. We'll be on the same campus."

"Really!" She lunged across the seat to kiss his cheek. "That's great. Maybe we can move in—"

"We'll see."

"Okay, now I'm so excited I'm scaring myself!" She laughed.

Beyond a stand of pines, golden light shimmered.

"We're here." He pulled the truck over to the side of the road and parked in front of Rio and Sela's cabin. The glow of a lit porch provided a visual oasis of peace.

Rio stood on the front steps, holding a wrapped bundle in his arms. Lifting a finger to lips, he made a hushing motion.

They climbed out of the truck and closed the doors as softly as possible.

Mitchell reached the steps first. He beamed as he

gave Rio a congratulatory pat on the shoulder. "Can I see him?" He spoke in a husky whisper.

Rio tugged the blanket away, revealing a beautiful sleeping baby with a head of dark hair.

With a gentle touch, Mitchell traced a fingertip across the baby's forehead. "He sure looks like a Waya. Do you think he's one of us?" Biting his lip. "You know what I mean. A Wolf?"

With a proud smile, Rio tilted the baby toward her so she good get a better look. "Too early to tell. It wouldn't make any difference to me one way or another. I'm so in love with this little guy, it's insane."

Mitchell grinned. "I'm happy for you and Sela."

Rio nodded toward the cabin. "Sela's asleep. There'll be some coffee and fry bread in the kitchen when you get back."

"It won't be before dawn." Mitchell wrapped his arm around her waist and drew her to his side. "I want to shift, take a long wolf run, and then show Christy Gray Paw Ridge."

"Great idea." Rio leaned close and kissed her cheek. "Best wishes, Christy, with your first shift. Welcome to the Black Hills pack." He glanced at Mitchell. "You'll be fine. You're in good hands."

Rising on tiptoe, she brushed a kiss to Rio's cheek. "I know I am."

"By the way," Rio whispered, "there's a greeting party in the ravine. Drew and Betty, Jace, and Michelle, of course, Ravage and Adrie, and probably a few others wanted to welcome Christy into the pack shifter or human as Mitchell's mate."

A lump rose in her throat. "Thank you."

The baby started to fuss.

Rio nodded. "I better go inside."

Mitchell led her by the hand past the cabin and along a dirt path to a trailhead marked with a stack of stones.

Feeling a rush of anticipation. "Where does this go?"

"It's a forested ravine with a stream running through it. It's the perfect place for a first shift. There's water to drink, plenty of trees to run through, and it's safe. We can play and howl all we want, and the sound won't carry."

The trail was shadowy, but her eyes adjusted in an instant. They hiked deep into the ravine. Boulders and tall trees surrounded them. Mitchell held her hand, lending a sense of reassurance. "What time is moon rise?"

"In about an hour. You'll be amazed. Through wolf eyes, dark woods will look like daylight. Close to the river, smells will be stronger, more interesting. Anything you taste or touch will be amplified. It might be overwhelming at first, but I hope you'll come to love a wolf-shift as much as I do."

"Anything we do together will be great."

Mitchell led her into a circle of trees. "We can undress and leave our clothes here."

Leaning against a tree, she pulled him close. Gazing into the starry sparkle in his eyes, she unfastened the buttons of his shirt one at a time, baring a silky triangle of hair. She skimmed her fingertips over his warm skin. "You have the most beautiful chest."

His soft breath near her ear tickled. "I could say the same about you."

"Kiss me."

He tangled his fingers in her hair and pressed

her against the rough bark of the trunk. His lips hovered a whisper of a touch from hers. "If I start kissing you now, I won't be able to stop."

"Promise." She giggled.

"I want us to shift first and take a wild run together to bond as wolf mates. Then shift back and make love as a man and woman who shared a special experience only they understand. Does that sound like a plan?"

Her heart pounded. "That's a mighty fine plan."

Tugging his boots off. "Okay! Let's do this."

A sense of exhilaration overrode any self-consciousness as she stripped her clothing and stacked it into a neat pile. She stood naked and giddy with laughter. "Thank you."

Mitchell stripped his jeans down his powerful thighs. "For what?"

"Saving me twice and sharing the blood-gift." She offered her hand. "God, I'm so nervous, I'm shaking. I'm scared I won't be able to shift."

"There's nothing to worry about." He enfolded her in his arms. "Shifter or human, I love you."

His bare skin brushed the length of her. The tiny hairs on his legs tickled her thighs. The faint scent of his musk intoxicated her senses.

"Close your eyes and take a deep breath." Mitchell's voice was calm. "The blood is already in your veins. It saved your life and healed you. Let your thoughts return to the wolf-dreams. It's that easy. Shifting is remembering what you are at heart. You've changed. You're a Wolf like me. Now relax and allow your body to shift."

"Will it hurt?"

"Maybe. Or it could go the other way and turn

into the biggest, baddest, adrenaline rush imaginable. Those shifts are good." His palm smoothed her hair. "Try not to think. Your body knows what to do. Shift with me."

"Look." His eyes flashed amber and tipped at a steeper angle. Dark fur covered his face. Mitchell began to take on a distinctly canine look.

Her heart raced. A light sheen of sweat broke over her skin. She knelt and watched in astonishment as her fingers turned to furred paws and scraped at a layer of pine needles. The transformation to Wolf felt wonderful. A fiery sting spread through her limbs as keen as having the sun detonate in her belly. Love for Mitchell and white-hot gratitude for the experience blasted every cell. In her mind, she shouted, *Wow! Wow! Wow!* But a wild howl poured out of her instead.

Mitchell shifted to wolf form. He playfully nipped at the fur around her throat. Glancing over her shoulder, she saw she had a lush coat and a bushy tail. She'd transformed to a Black Hills Wolf, too.

Mitchell darted away to chase shadows, and she followed, howling with joy.

Hoooowl! Other wolves in the ravine answered back in welcome.

About the Author

Katalina Leon is an artist and author who can't commit to a single romance subgenre. Her favorite playgrounds are historical, Sci-fi, contemporary, and most of all paranormal realms. Lately, she has wolf-shifters on the brain. Katalina brings a sense of adventure and a touch of the mystical to erotic romance. She believes there's a daring heroine inside every woman who wants to take a wild ride with a strong worthy hero.

AuthorClassified's, 2015 Romantic Suspense Author of the Year.
Join my newsletter for freebies ARCs and the latest releases.
Sign-up for my newsletter here:
http://eepurl.com/bzR1d9

https://www.facebook.com/katalinaleonauthor

http://www.katalinaleon.com

Also by Katalina

Portrait of a Lone Wolf
The Virgin and Her Wolf